A Cowboy's Wish Upon a Star

—

Caro Carson

D0044026

⬥ HARLEQUIN®SPECIAL EDITION®

Recycling programs
for this product may
not exist in your area.

ISBN-13: 978-0-373-65097-2

A Cowboy's Wish Upon a Star

Copyright © 2016 by Caro Carson

HARLEQUIN®
™ www.Harlequin.com

Printed in U.S.A.

"You have to get the groceries for me."

"Nope. It's May." He stuck his hat on, so his hands were free to pick up his second boot and shake the cell phone out of it.

"It's May? What kind of answer is that? Do you fast in May or do a colon cleanse or something?"

He looked up at her joke, but his grin died before it started. Judging by the look on her face, she wasn't joking. "The River Mack rounds up in May."

She looked at him, waiting. He realized a woman from Hollywood probably had no idea what that meant.

"We're busy. We're branding. We have to keep an eye on the late calving, the bulls—"

He stopped himself. He wasn't going to explain the rest. Managing a herd was a constant, complex operation.

Sophia flapped one hand toward the kitchen behind her. "I have nothing to eat. You have to help me."

He stomped into his second boot. "Not unless you're a pregnant or nursing cow."

At her gasp, he did laugh. "I keep every beast on this ranch fed, but you, ma'am, are not a beast. You're a movie star, a woman who can take care of herself, and you're not my problem."

She looked absolutely stricken. Had he been so harsh?

"Listen, if I'm going toward town, I don't mind picking you up a gallon of milk. That's just common courtesy. I expect you to do the same for me."

"I can't leave the ranch."

"Neither can I. Now if you'll excuse me, I've got a barn full of animals to feed before I can feed myself."

TEXAS RESCUE:
Rescuing hearts...one Texan at a time!

Dear Reader,

The wonderful Jane Austen once wrote that the heroine of her book *Emma* was a woman "whom no-one but myself will much like." I confess, I'm feeling the same way about the heroine of the book you are holding in your hand at this moment.

Sophia Jackson, like the wealthy heiress Emma, seems to have it all. She's a movie star. She's gorgeous. At just twenty-nine years of age, she's achieved a high level of success. But Sophia is not living as charmed a life as it appears. In fact, her life is falling apart, and she knows it's the result of her own carelessness and bad choices. She doesn't believe she really deserves to have good things happen to her anymore—and so she makes everything worse before it gets better.

At the heart of her insecurity is an unexpected pregnancy. I think readers who are parents will identify with the anxiety that comes with a first pregnancy. How do you know if you have what it takes to raise a baby? I thought the hospital was crazy to let me leave with my first newborn; wasn't it obvious that my husband and I were clueless?

Fortunately, we figured things out, as most new parents do. In this book, Sophia Jackson must figure out what's best for her coming baby, for her life and, most of all, for the man she falls madly in love with. And I hope you, dear reader, will like Sophia as much as I do by the last page!

Cheers,

Caro Carson

Despite a no-nonsense background as a West Point graduate and US Army officer, **Caro Carson** has always treasured the happily-ever-after of a good romance novel. Now Caro is delighted to be living her own happily-ever-after with her husband and two children in the great state of Florida, a location that has saved the coaster-loving theme-park fanatic a fortune on plane tickets.

Books by Caro Carson

Harlequin Special Edition

Montana Mavericks:
What Happened at the Wedding?

The Maverick's Holiday Masquerade

Texas Rescue

Her Texas Rescue Doctor
Following Doctor's Orders
A Texas Rescue Christmas
Not Just a Cowboy

The Doctors MacDowell

The Bachelor Doctor's Bride
The Doctor's Former Fiancée
Doctor, Soldier, Daddy

Visit the Author Profile page
at Harlequin.com for more titles.

This book is dedicated to You,
the reader who
spent time to meet me at the book signing,
or spent time to send me the note to say
you love the love stories that
I spent time to write.
Thank you.

Chapter One

It was the end of the world.

Sophia Jackson strained to see something, anything that looked like civilization, but the desolate landscape was no more than brown dirt and scrubby bits of green plants that stretched all the way to the horizon.

She might have been in one of her own movies.

The one that had garnered an Academy Award nomination for her role as a dying frontier woman had been filmed in Mexico, but this part of Texas looked close enough. The one that had made her an overnight success as a Golden Globe winner for her portrayal of a doomed woman in a faraway galaxy had been filmed in Italy, but again, this landscape was eerily similar.

Doomed. Dying. Isolated.

She'd channeled those emotions before. This time, however, no one was going to yell *cut*. No one was going to hand her a gold statue.

"Are we there yet?" She sounded demanding, just like the junior officer thrust into a leadership role on a space colony.

Well, not really. She had the ear of an actor; she could catch nuance in tone and delivery, even in—or especially in—her own voice. She didn't sound like a commander. She sounded like a diva.

I have the right to be a diva. I've got the gold statue to prove it.

She tossed her hair back with a jingle of her chandelier earrings, queen of the backseat of the car.

In the front bucket seats, her sister's fiancé continued to drive down the endless road in silence, but Sophia caught the quick glance he shared with her sister. The two of them didn't think she was a young military officer. They didn't even think of her as a diva.

She was an annoying, spoiled brat who was going to be dropped off in the middle of abso-freaking-lutely nowhere.

Her sister, Grace, reached back between the seats to pat her on the knee. "I haven't been here before, either, but it can't be too much farther. Isn't it perfect, though? The paparazzi will never find you out here. This is just what we were hoping for."

Sophia looked at Grace's hand as it patted the black leather which covered her knee. Grace's engagement ring was impossible to miss. Her sister had been her rock, her constant companion, until very recently. Now, wearing a different kind of rock on her left hand, Grace was giddy at the prospect of marrying the man who'd encouraged her to dump her own sister.

Sophia mentally stuck out her tongue at the back of the man's head. Her future brother-in-law was a stupid doctor named Alex, and he'd never once been impressed with Sophia Jackson, movie star. Since the day Sophia and Grace had arrived in Texas, he'd only paid attention to Grace.

Grace's hand moved from Sophia's knee to Alex's shoulder. Then to the back of his neck. The diamond played peek-a-boo as her sister slid her hand through her fiancé's dark hair.

Sophia looked away, out the side window to the desolate horizon. The nausea was rising, so she chomped on her chewing gum. Loudly. With no class. No elegance. None of the grace that the world had once expected of the talented Sophia Jackson.

Pun intended. I have no Grace, not anymore.

Grace didn't correct her gum-smacking. Grace no longer cared enough to correct her.

Sophia was on her own. She'd have to survive the rest of her nine-month sentence all by herself, hiding from the world. In the end, all she'd have to show for it would be a flabby stomach and stretch marks. Like a teenager in the last century, she was pregnant and ashamed, terrified of being exposed. She had to be sent to the country to hide until she could have the baby, give it up for adoption, and then return to the world and spend the rest of her life pretending nothing had ever happened.

If she had a world to return to. That was a very big *if*.

No one in Hollywood would work with her. It had nothing to do with the pregnancy. No one knew about that, and she wasn't far enough along to even begin to show. No, the world of movie stardom was boxing her out solely because of her reputation.

A box office giant, an actor whom Sophia had always dreamed of working with, had recently informed a major studio he would not do the picture if she were cast opposite him. Her reputation had sunk that low. They said there was no such thing as bad publicity, but the publicity she'd been generating had hurt her. Her publicist and her agent had each informed her that she was unmarketable as is.

Ex-publicist. Ex-agent. They both left me.

Panic crawled up the back of her throat. They were all leaving her. Publicist, agent, that louse of a slimy boyfriend she'd been stupid enough to run away with. And worst of all, within the next few minutes, her sister. She was losing the best personal assistant in the world, right when she needed a personal assistant the most.

There was no such thing as loyalty in Hollywood. Not even her closest blood relative was standing by her side. Nausea turned to knots.

"Oh, my goodness," her sister laughed. The tone was one of happy, happy surprise.

Alex's laugh was masculine, amused. "Just in case you needed a reminder that you're in the middle of a genuine Texas cattle ranch..."

He brought their car to a stop—as if he had a choice. The view through the windshield was now the bulky brown back of a giant steer. A thousand pounds of animal blocked their way, just standing there on the road they needed to use, the road that would lead them to an empty ranch house where Sophia would be abandoned, alone, left behind.

Knots turned to panic. She needed to get this over with. Her world was going to end, and she couldn't drag this out one second longer.

Let's rip this bandage off.

"Move, you stupid cow!" she hollered from the backseat.

"Sophia, that's not going to help."

But Sophia had already half vaulted over Alex's shoulder and slammed her palm on the car horn. "Get out of the road."

The cow stared at her through the glass, unmoving.

God above, she was tired of being stared at. Everyone was always waiting for her to do something, to be crazy or brilliant, to act out every emotion while they watched passively. Grace was staring at her now, shaking her head.

"Move!" Sophia laid on the horn again.

"Stop it." Alex firmly took her arm and pushed her toward the backseat. His stare was more of a glare.

He and Grace both turned back toward the front. Sophia had spoiled their little delight at a cow in the road, at this unexpected interlude in their sweet, shared day.

I can't stand it, I can't stand myself, I can't stand this one more minute.

She yanked on the door handle and shoved the door open.

"Sophia! Stay in the car." Grace sounded equal parts exasperated and fearful.

Sophia was beyond fear. Panic, nausea, knots—a terrible need to get this over with. Once the ax fell, once she was cut off from the last remnants of her life, she could fall apart. She wanted nothing more than to fall apart, and this stupid cow was preventing it.

She slammed the car door and waved her arms over her head, advancing on the cow. Or maybe it was a bull. It had short horns. Whatever it was, it flinched.

Emboldened—or just plain crazy, like they all said—Sophia waved her arms over her head some more and advanced toward the stupid, stationary cow. The May weather was warm on the bare skin of her midriff as her crop top rose higher with each wave of her arms. On her second step, she nearly went down as her ankle twisted, the spike heel of her over-the-knee boot threatening to sink into the brown Texas dirt.

"Move, do you hear me? Move." She gestured wide to

the vast land all around them. "Anywhere. Anywhere but right here."

The cow snorted at her. Chewed something. Didn't care about her, didn't care about her at all.

Tears were spilling over her cheeks, Sophia realized suddenly. Her ankle hurt, her heart hurt, her stomach hurt. The cow looked away, not interested in the least. Being ignored was worse than being stared at. The beast was massive, far stockier than the horses she'd worked with on the set as a dying frontier woman. She shoved at the beast's shoulder anyway.

"Just *move!*" Its hide was coarse and dusty. She shoved harder, accomplishing nothing, feeling her own insignificance. She might as well not exist. No career, no sister, no friends, no life.

She collapsed on the thick, warm neck of the uncaring cow, and let the tears flow.

Someone on the ranch was in trouble.

Travis Chalmers tossed his pliers into the leather saddlebag and gave the barb wire one last tug. Fixed.

He scooped up his horse's trailing reins in one hand, smashed his cowboy hat more firmly over his brow, and swung into the saddle. That car horn meant something else needed fixing, and now. He only hoped one of his men hadn't been injured.

The car horn sounded again. Travis kicked the horse into a gallop, heading in the direction of the sound. It didn't sound like one of the ranch trucks' horns. A visitor, then, who could be lost, out of gas, stranded by a flat tire—simple fixes.

He kept his seat easily and let the horse have her head. Whatever the situation was, he'd handle it. He was young for a foreman, just past thirty, but he'd been ranching since the day he was born, seemed like. Nothing that happened on a cattle operation came as a surprise to him.

He rode up the low rise toward the road, and the cause of the commotion came into view. A heifer was standing in the road, blocking the path of a sports car that clearly wouldn't be able to handle any off-road terrain, so it couldn't go around the animal. That the animal was on the road wasn't a surprise; Travis had just repaired a gap in the barb wire fence. But leaning on the heifer, her back to him, was a woman.

What a woman, with long hair flowing perfectly down her back, her body lean and toned, her backside curvy—all easy to see because any skin that wasn't bared to the sun and sky was encased in tight black clothing. But it was her long legs in thigh-high boots that made him slow his horse in a moment of stunned confusion.

She had to be a mirage. No woman actually wore thigh-high leather boots with heels that high. Those boots sent sexual signals that triggered every adolescent memory of a comic book heroine. Half-naked, high-heeled—a character drawn to appeal to the most primal part of a man's mind.

Not much on a cattle ranch could surprise him, except seeing *that* in the middle of the road.

The horse continued toward the heifer, its focus absolute. So was Travis's. He couldn't take his eyes off the woman as he rode toward her.

She lifted her head and turned his way. With a dash of her cheek against her black-clad shoulder, she turned all the way around and leaned against the animal, stretching her arms along its back like it was her sofa. As the wind blew her hair back from her face, silver and gold shining in the sun, she held her pose and watched him come for her.

Boots, bare skin, black leather—they messed with his brain, until the car door opened and the driver began to get out, a man. Then the passenger door opened, too, and the heifer swung her head, catching the smell of horse and humans on the wind. The rancher in him pushed aside the adolescent male, and he returned his horse to a quicker lope with a *tch* and a press of his thigh.

That heifer wasn't harmless. Let her get nervous, and a half ton of beef on the hoof could do real harm to the humans crowding her, including the sex goddess in boots.

"Afternoon, folks." Travis took in the other two at a glance. Worried woman, irritated man. He didn't look at the goddess as he stopped near the strange little grouping. His heart had kicked into a higher gear at the sight of her, something the sound of the horn and the short gallop had not done. It was damned disconcerting. Everything about her was disconcerting. "Stay behind those doors, if you don't mind."

"Sophia, it's time to get back in the car now," the man said, exaggeratedly patient and concerned, as if he were talking a jumper off a ledge.

"No."

"Oh, Sophie." The woman gave the smallest shake of her head, her eyes sad. Apparently, this Sophie had disappointed her before.

Sophie. Sophia. He looked at her again. Sophia Jackson, of course. Unmistakable. A movie star on his ranch, resting against his heifer, a scenario so bizarre his brain had to work to believe his eyes.

She hadn't taken her blue eyes off him, but she'd raised her chin in challenge. The *no* was meant for him, was it?

"Walk away," he said mildly, keeping his voice even for the heifer's benefit—and hers. "I'll get this heifer on her way so you can get on yours."

"No. She likes me." Sophia's long, elegant fingers stroked the roan hide of the cattle.

"Is that right?" He reached back to grab his lasso and held the loops in one hand.

"My cow doesn't want to leave me. She's loyal and true."

It was an absurd thing to say. Travis didn't have time for absurd.

"Watch your toes." He rode forward, crowding the heifer, crowding Sophia Jackson, and slapped the heifer on the hindquarters with the coiled rope. She briskly left the road.

Sophia Jackson looked a little smaller and a lot sillier, standing in the road by herself. He looked down at her famous face as she watched the heifer leave. She actually looked sad, like she didn't want the heifer to go, which was as absurd as everything else about the situation.

Travis wheeled his horse away from Sophia in order to talk to the driver.

"Where are you heading?"

"Thanks for moving that animal. I'm Alex Gregory. This is my fiancée, Grace."

Travis waited, but the man didn't introduce the woman in boots. He guessed he was supposed to recognize her. He did. Still, it seemed rude to leave her out.

"Travis Chalmers." He touched the brim of his hat and nodded at the worried woman, then twisted halfway around in his saddle to touch his hat and nod again at the movie star in their midst.

"Chalmers, the foreman?" asked the man, Alex. "Good to meet you. The MacDowells told me they'd explained the situation to you."

Not exactly.

Travis hooked his lasso onto the saddle horn. "You're the one who's gonna live in Marion MacDowell's house for a few months?"

"No, not us. Her. Sophia is my fiancée's sister. She needs a place to hide."

He raised a brow at the word. "Hide from what?"

"Paparazzi," Grace answered. "It's been a real issue after the whole debacle with the—well, it's always an issue. But Sophie needs some time to…to…" She smiled with kindness and pity at her sister. "She needs some time."

Sophie stalked around the car on spiked heels, looking like a warrior queen who could kick some serious butt, but instead she got in the backseat and slammed the door.

"Time and privacy," Alex added. "The MacDowells assured us your discretion wouldn't be an issue."

His mare shifted under him and blew an impatient breath through her nose.

"Should we go to the house and have this discussion there?" Grace asked.

Travis kept an eye on the heifer that was ambling away. "I'm gonna have to round up that heifer and put her back on the right side of the fence. Got to check on the branding after that, but I'll be back at sundown. I go past the main house on the way to my place. I'll stop in."

"We weren't planning to stay all day." The woman threw a look of dismay to her fiancé.

They couldn't expect him to quit working in the middle of the day and go sit in a house to chat. He ran the River Mack ranch, and that meant he worked even longer hours than he expected from his ranch hands.

Heifers that wandered through broken fences couldn't be put off until tomorrow. May was one of the busiest months of the year, between the last of the calving and the bulk of the branding. Travis hadn't planned on spending any time whatsoever talking to whomever the MacDowells were loaning their house, but obviously, there was more to the situation than the average houseguest.

"All right, then. Let's talk." He swung himself off the horse, a concession to let them know they had his time and attention. Besides, if he stayed on horseback, he couldn't see Sophia in the car. It felt like he needed to keep an eye on her, the same as he needed to do with the wandering heifer.

On the ground, he still couldn't see much through the windshield. He caught a glimpse of black leather, her hands resting on her knees. Her hands were clenched into fists.

Travis shook his head. She was a woman on edge.

"Sophia just needs to be left alone," her sister said.

"I can do that." He had no intention of staying in the vicinity of someone as disturbing to his peace of mind as that woman.

"If men with cameras start snooping around, please, tell them nothing. Don't even deny she's here."

"Ma'am, if men with cameras come snooping around this ranch, I will be escorting them off the property."

"Oh, really? You can do that?" She seemed relieved—amazed and relieved.

What did these people expect? He took his hat off and ran his hand through his hair before shoving the hat right back on again. His hair was getting too long, but no cowboy had time in May to go into town and see a barber.

"We don't tolerate trespassers," he explained to the people who clearly lived in town. "I'm not in the business of distinguishing between cameramen and cattle thieves. If you don't belong here, you will be escorted off the land."

"The paparazzi will offer you money, though. Thousands."

Before Travis could set her straight on this insinuation that he could be bribed to betray a guest of the MacDowells, Alex cut in. "That's only if they find her. We've gone to great lengths to arrange this location. We took away her cell phone so that she wouldn't accidentally store a photo in the cloud with a location stamp. Hackers get paid to look for things like that. That's how extreme the hunting for her can be."

"She's got a burner phone for emergencies," Grace said. "But if you could check on her...?"

Travis was aware that the front doors to the car were wide open, man and woman each standing beside one. Surely, the subject of this conversation could hear every word. It seemed rude to talk about her as if she weren't there.

"If she wants me to check on her, I will. If she wants me to leave her alone, I will."

He looked through the windshield again. The fists had disappeared. One leather-clad knee was being bounced, jittery, impatient.

"How many other people work on this ranch?" the man asked.

"Will they leave my sister alone?" the woman asked.

Travis was feeling impatient himself. This whole conversation was moving as far from his realm of normal as the woman hiding in the car was.

That was what she was doing in there. Rather than being part of a conversation about herself, she was hiding. This was all a lot of nonsense in the middle of branding season, but from long habit developed by working with animals, Travis forced himself to stand calmly, keep the reins loose in his hands, and not show his irritation. These people were strangers in the middle of the road, and Travis owed them nothing.

"I'm not in the habit of discussing the ranch's staffing requirements with strangers."

The man nodded once. He got it. The woman bit her

lip, and Travis understood she was worried about more than herself.

"But since this is your sister, I'll tell you the amount of ranch hands living in the bunkhouse varies depending on the season. None of us are in the habit of going to the main house to introduce ourselves to Mrs. MacDowell's houseguests." Travis spoke clearly, to be sure the woman in the car heard him. "If your sister doesn't want to be seen, then I suggest she stop standing in the middle of an open pasture and hugging my livestock."

The black boot stopped bouncing.

Grace dipped her chin to hide her smile, looking as pretty as her movie star sister—minus the blatant sexuality.

"Now if you folks would like to head on to the house, I've got to be going."

"Thank you," Grace said, but the worry returned to her expression. "If you could check on her, though, yourself? She's more fragile than she looks. She's got a lot of decisions weighing her down. This is a very delicate situa—"

The car horn ripped through the air. Travis nearly lost the reins as his mare instinctively made to bolt without him. *Goddammit.*

No sooner had he gotten his horse's head under control than the horn blasted again. He whipped his own head around toward the car, glaring at the two adults who were still standing there. For God's sake, did they have to be told to shut her up?

"Tell her to stop."

"Like that'll do any good." But the man bent to look into the car. "Enough, Sophie."

"Sophie, please..."

One more short honk. Thank God his horse trusted him, because the mare barely flinched this time, but it was the last straw for Travis. Reins in hand, he stalked past the man and yanked open the rear door.

Since she'd been leaning forward to reach the car horn, Sophia's black-clad backside was the first thing he saw, but she quickly turned toward him, keeping her arm stretched toward the steering wheel.

"Don't do that again."

"Quit standing around talking about me. This is a waste of time. I want to get to the house. Now." She honked the horn again, staring right at him as she did it.

"What the hell is wrong with you? I just said don't do that."

"Or else what?"

She glared at him like a warrior, but she had the attitude of a kindergartner.

"Every time you honk that horn, another cowboy on this ranch drops what he's doing to come and see if you need help. It's not a game. It's a call for help."

She blinked. Clearly, she hadn't thought of that, but then she narrowed her eyes and reached once more for the steering wheel.

"You honk that horn again, and you will very shortly find the road blocked by men on horses, and we will not move until you turn the car around and take yourself right back to wherever it is you came from."

Her hand hovered over the steering wheel.

"Do it," he said. "Frighten my horse one more time. You will never set foot on this ranch again."

Her hand hovered. He stared her down, waiting, almost willing her to test him. He would welcome a chance to remove her from the ranch, and he wasn't a man to make empty threats.

"I don't want to be here, anyway," she said.

He jerked his head toward the steering wheel. "You

know how to drive, don't you? Turn the car around then, instead of honking that damned horn."

The silence stretched between them.

Her sister had leaned into the car, so she spoke very softly. "Sophie, you've got nowhere else to go. You cannot live with me and Alex."

Travis saw it then. Saw the way the light in Sophia's eyes died a little, saw the way her breath left her lips. He saw her pain, and he was sorry for it.

She sagged back into her seat, burying her backside along with the rest of her body in the corner. She crossed her arms over her middle, not looking at her sister, not looking at him. "Well, God forbid I should piss off a horse."

Travis stood and shut the door. He scanned the pasture, spotted the heifer twice as far away as she'd been a minute ago. Those young ones had a sixth sense about getting rounded up, sometimes. If they didn't want to be penned in, they were twice as hard to catch.

Didn't matter. Travis hadn't met one yet that could outsmart or outrun him.

He had a heifer to catch, branding to oversee, a ranch to run. By the time the sun went down, he'd want nothing more than a hot shower and a flat surface to sleep on.

But tonight, he'd stop by the main house and check on a movie star—a sad, angry movie star who had nowhere else to go, no other family to take her in. Nowhere except his ranch.

With a nod at the sister and her fiancé, Travis swung himself back into the saddle. The heifer had given up all pretense at grazing and was determinedly trotting toward the horizon, putting distance between herself and the humans.

Travis would have sighed, if cowboys sighed. Instead,

he spoke to his horse under his breath. "You ready for this?"

He pointed the mare toward the heifer and sent her into motion with a squeeze of his thigh. They had a long, hard ride ahead.

Chapter Two

She was alone.

She was alone, and she was going to die, because Grace and Alex had left her, and even though Alex had flipped a bunch of fuses and turned on the electricity, and even though Grace had carried in two bags of groceries from the car and set them on the blue-tiled kitchen counter, Sophia's only family had abandoned her before anyone realized the refrigerator was broken, and now the food was going to spoil and they wouldn't be back to check on her for a week and by then she'd be dead from starvation, her body on the kitchen floor, her eyes staring sightlessly at the wallpaper border with its white geese repeated ad nauseam on a dull blue background.

Last year, she'd worn Givenchy as she made her acceptance speech.

I hate my life.

Sophia sat at the kitchen table in a hard chair and cried.

No one yelled *cut*, so she continued the scene, putting her elbows on the table and dropping her head in her hands.

I hate myself for letting this become my life.

Was that what Grace and Alex wanted her to come to grips with? That she'd messed up her own life?

Well, duh, I'm not a moron. I know exactly why my career is circling the drain in a slow death spiral.

Because no one wanted to work with her. And no one wanted to work with her because no one liked her ex, DJ Deezee Kalm.

Kalm was something of an ironic name for the jerk. Deezee had brought nothing but chaos into her life since she'd met him…wow, only five months ago?

Five months ago, Sophia Jackson had been the Next Big Thing. No longer had she needed to beg for a chance to audition for secondary characters. Scripts from the biggest and the best were being delivered to her door by courier, with affectionate little notes suggesting the main character would fit her perfectly.

Sophia and her sister—her loyal, faithful assistant—had deserved a chance to celebrate. After ten long years of hard work, Sophia's dreams were coming true, but if she was being honest with herself—*and isn't that what this time alone is supposed to be about? Being honest with myself?*—well, to be honest, she might have acted elated, but she'd been exhausted.

A week in Telluride, a tiny mining town that was now a millionaires' playground in the Rocky Mountains, had seemed like a great escape. For one little week, she wouldn't worry about the future impact of her every decision. Sophia would be seen, but maybe she wouldn't be stared at among the rich and famous.

But DJ Deezee Kalm had noticed her. Sophia had been a sucker for his lies, and now she couldn't be seen by anyone at all for the next nine months. Here she was, alone with her thoughts and some rapidly thawing organic frozen meals, the kind decorated with chia seeds and labeled with exotic names from India.

There you go. I fell for a jerk, and now I hate my life. Reflection complete.

She couldn't dwell on Deezee, not without wanting to throw something. If she chucked the goose-shaped salt shaker against the wall, she'd probably never be able to replace the 1980s ceramic. That was the last thing she needed: the guilt of destroying some widow's hideous salt shaker.

She stood with the vague idea that she ought to do something about the paper bags lined up on the counter, but her painful ankle made fresh tears sting her eyes. She'd twisted it pretty hard in the dirt road when she'd confronted that cow, although she'd told Alex the Stupid Doctor that she hadn't. She sat down again and began unzipping the boots to free her toes from their spike-heeled torture.

That cow in the road…she hoped it had given that cowboy a run for his money. She hoped it was still outrunning him right this second, Mr. Don't-Honk-That-Horn-or-Else. Now that she thought about it, he'd had perfect control of his horse as he'd galloped away from them like friggin' Indiana Jones in a Spielberg film, so he'd lied to her about the horn upsetting his horse. Liar, liar. Typical man.

Don't trust men. Lesson learned. Can I go back to LA now?

But no. She couldn't. She was stuck here in Texas, where Grace had dragged her to make an appearance on behalf of the Texas Rescue and Relief organization. Her sister had hoped charity work and good deeds could repair the damage Sophia had done to her reputation. Instead, in the middle of just such a big charity event, Deezee had shown up and publicly begged Sophia to take him back. Sophia had been a sucker again. With cameras dogging their every move, she'd run away to a Caribbean island with him, an elopement that had turned out to be a big joke.

Ha, ha, ha.

Here's something funny, Deezee. When I peed on a plastic stick, a little plus sign showed up.

Sophia had returned from St. Barth to find her sister engaged to a doctor with Texas Rescue, a man who, unlike Deezee, seemed to take that engagement seriously. Now her sister never wanted to go back to LA with her, because Alex had her totally believing in fairy tale love. Grace believed Texas would be good for Sophia, too. Living here would give her a chance to rest and *relax*.

Right. Because of that little plus sign, Grace thought Sophia needed some stress-free *alone time* to decide what she wanted to do with her future, as if Sophia had done anything except worry about both of their futures for the past ten years. Didn't Grace know Sophia was sick of worrying about the future?

Barefooted, Sophia went to the paper bags and pulled out all the cold and wet items and stuck them in the sink. They'd already started sweating on the tiled countertop. She dried her cheek on her shoulder and faced the fridge.

It had been deliberately turned off by the owner, a woman who didn't want to stay in Texas and *relax* in her own home now that her kids were grown and married. Before abandoning her house to spend a year volunteering for a medical mission in Africa, Mrs. MacDowell had inserted little plastic wedges to keep the doors open so the refrigerator wouldn't get moldy and funky while it was unused.

Sophia was going to be moldy and funky by the time they found her starved body next week. She had a phone for emergencies; she used it.

"Grace? It's me. Alex didn't turn the refrigerator on." Sophia felt betrayed. Her voice only sounded bitchy.

"Sophie, sweetie, that's not an emergency." Grace spoke gently, like someone chiding a child and trying to encourage her at the same time. "You can handle that. You know how to flip a switch in a fuse box."

"I don't even know where the fuse box is."

Grace sighed, and Sophia heard her exchange a few words with Alex. "It's in the hall closet. I've gotta run now. Bye."

"Wait! Just hang on the line with me while I find the fuse box. What if the fuse doesn't fix it?"

"I don't know. Then you'll have to call a repairman, I guess."

"Call a repairman?" Sophia was aghast. "Where would I even find a repairman?"

"There's a phone on the wall in the kitchen. Mrs. Mac-Dowell has a phone book sitting on the little stand underneath it."

Sophia looked around the 1980s time capsule of a kitchen. Sure enough, mounted on the wall was a phone, one with a handset and a curly cord hanging down. It was not decorated with a goose, but it was white, to fit in the decor.

"Ohmigod, that's an antique."

"I made sure it works. It's a lot harder for paparazzi to tap an actual phone line than it would be for them to use a scanner to listen in to this phone call. You can call a repairman."

Sophia clenched her jaw against that lecturing tone. From the day her little sister had graduated from high school, Sophia had paid her to take care of details like this, treating her like a star's personal assistant long before Sophia had been a star. Now Grace had decided to dump her.

"And how am I supposed to pay for a repairman?"

"You have a credit card. We put it in my name, but it's yours." Grace sounded almost sad. Pitying her, actually, with just a touch of impatience in her tone.

Sophia felt her sister slipping away. "I can say my name is Grace, but I can't change my face. How am I supposed to stay anonymous if a repairman shows up at the door?"

"I don't know, Sophie. Throw a dish towel over your head or something."

"You don't care about me anymore." Her voice should have broken in the middle of that sentence, because her heart was breaking, but the actor inside knew the line had been delivered in a continuous whine.

"I love you, Sophie. You'll figure something out. You're super smart. You took care of me for years. This will be a piece of cake for you."

A piece of cake. That tone of voice…

Oh, God, her sister sounded just like their mother. Ten years ago, Mom and Dad had been yanked away from them forever, killed in a pointless car accident. At nineteen, Sophia had become the legal guardian of Grace, who'd still had two years of high school left to go.

Nothing had been a piece of cake. Sophia had quit college and moved back home so that Grace could finish high school in their hometown. Sophia had needed to make the life insurance last, paying the mortgage with it during Grace's junior and senior years. She'd tried to supplement it with modeling jobs, but anything local only paid a pittance. For fifty dollars, she'd spent six hours gesturing toward a mattress with a smile on her face.

It had really been her first acting job, because during the entire photo shoot, she'd had to act like she wasn't mourning the theater scholarship at UCLA that she'd sacrificed.

With a little sister to raise, making a mattress look desirable was as close as Sophia could come to show business.

That first modeling job had been a success, eventually used nationwide, but Sophia hadn't been paid one penny more. Her flat fifty-dollar fee had been spent on gas and groceries that same day. Grace had to be driven to school. Grace had to eat lunch in the cafeteria.

Now Grace was embarking on her own happy life and leaving Sophia behind. It just seemed extra cruel that Grace would sound like Mom at this point.

"I have to run," her mother's voice said. "I love you, Sophie. You can do this. Bye."

Don't leave me. Don't ever leave me. I miss you.

The phone was silent.

This afternoon, Sophia had only wanted to hide away and fall apart in private. Now, she was terrified to. If she started crying again, she would never, ever stop.

She nearly ran to the hall closet and pushed aside the old coats and jackets to find the fuse box. They were all on, a neat row of black switches all pointing to the left. She flicked a few to the right, then left again. Then a few more. If she reset every one, then she would have to hit the one that worked the refrigerator.

It made no difference. The refrigerator was still dead when she returned to the kitchen. The food was still thawing in the sink. Her life still sucked, only worse now, because now she missed her mother all over again. Grace sounded like Mom, and she'd left her like Mom. At least when Mom had died, she'd left the refrigerator running.

What a terrible thing to think. Dear God, she hated herself.

Then she laughed at the incredible low her self-pity could reach.

Then she cried.

Just as she'd known it would, once the crying started, it did not stop.

I'm pregnant and I'm scared and I want my mother.

Sophia sank to the kitchen floor, hugged her knees to her chest, and gave up.

Would he or wouldn't he?

Travis rode slowly, letting his mare cool down on her way to the barn while he debated with himself whether or not he'd told the sister he would check on the movie star tonight, specifically, or just check on her in general. He was bone-tired and hungry, but he had almost another mile to go before he could rest. Half a mile to the barn, quarter of a mile past that to his house. A movie star with an attitude was the last thing he wanted to deal with. Tomorrow would be soon enough to be neighborly and ask how she was settling in.

The MacDowell house, or just *the house*, as everyone on a ranch traditionally called the owner's residence, was closer to the barn than his own. As the mare walked on, the house's white porch pillars came into view, always a pretty sight. The sunset tinted the sky pink and orange behind it. Mesquite trees were spaced evenly around it. The lights were on; Sophia Jackson was home.

Then the lights went out.

On again.

What the hell?

Lights started turning off and on, in an orderly manner, left to right across the building. Travis had been in the house often enough that he knew which window was the living room. Off, on. The dining room. The foyer.

The mare chomped at her bit impatiently, picking up on his change in mood.

"Yeah, girl. Go on." He let the horse pick up her pace.

Normally, he'd never let a horse hurry back to the barn; that was just sure to start a bad habit. But everything on the River Mack was his responsibility, including the house with its blinking lights, and its new resident.

The lights came on and stayed on as he rode steadily toward the movie star that he was going to check on tonight, after all.

Chapter Three

Travis couldn't ride his horse up to the front door and leave her on the porch. There was a hitching post on the side that faced the barn, so he rode around the house toward the back. The kitchen door was the one everyone used, anyway.

The first year he'd landed a job here as a ranch hand, he'd learned real quick to leave the barn through the door that faced the house. Mrs. MacDowell was as likely as not to open her kitchen door and call over passing ranch hands to see if they'd help her finish off something she'd baked. She was forever baking Bundt cakes and what not, then insisting she couldn't eat them before they went stale. Since her sons had all gone off to medical school to become doctors, Travis suspected she just didn't know how to stop feeding young men. As a twenty-five-year-old living in the bunkhouse on canned pork-n-beans, he'd been happy to help her not let anything get stale.

Travis grinned at the memory. From the vantage point of his horse's back, he looked down into the kitchen as he passed its window and saw another woman there. Blond hair, black clothes...curled up on the floor. Weeping.

"Whoa," he said softly, and the mare stopped.

He could tell in a glance Sophia Jackson wasn't hurt, the same way he could tell in a glance if a cowboy who'd been thrown from a horse was hurt. She could obviously breathe if she could cry. She was hugging her knees to her chest in a way that proved she didn't have any broken bones. As he watched, she shook that silver and gold hair back and got to her feet, her back to him. She could move just fine. There was nothing he needed to fix.

She was emotional, but Travis couldn't fix that. There wasn't a lot of weeping on a cattle ranch. If a youngster got homesick out on a roundup or a heartbroken cowboy shed a tear over a Dear John letter after a mail call, Travis generally kept an eye on them from a distance. Once they'd regained their composure, he'd find some reason to check in with them, asking about their saddle or if they'd noticed the creek was low. If they cared to talk, they were welcome to bring it up. Some did. Most didn't.

He'd give Sophia Jackson her space, then. Whatever was making her sad, it was hers to cry over. Tomorrow night would be soon enough to check in with her.

Just as he nudged his horse back into a walk, he caught a movement out of the corner of his eye, Sophia dashing her cheek on her shoulder. He tried to put it out of his mind once he was in the barn, but it nagged at him as he haltered his mare and washed off her bit. Sophia had touched her cheek to her shoulder just like that when he'd first approached her on the road this afternoon. Had she been crying when she'd hung on to that heifer?

He rubbed his jaw. In the car, she'd been all clenched

fists and anxiously bouncing knee. A woman on the edge, that was what he'd thought. Looked like she'd gone over that edge this evening.

People did. Not his problem. There were limits to what a foreman was expected to handle, damn it.

But the way she'd been turning the lights off and on was odd. What did that have to do with being sad?

His mare nudged him in the shoulder, unhappy with the way he was standing still.

"I know, I know. I have to go check on her." He turned the mare into the paddock so she could enjoy the last of the twilight without a saddle on her back, then turned himself toward the house. It was only about a hundred yards from barn to kitchen door, an easy walk over hard-packed earth to a wide flagstone patio that held a couple of wooden picnic tables. The kitchen door was protected by its original small back porch and an awning.

A hundred yards was far enough to give Travis time to think about how long he'd been in the saddle today, how long he'd be in the saddle tomorrow, and how he was hungry enough to eat his hat.

He took his hat off and knocked at the back door.

No answer.

He knocked again. His stomach growled.

"Go away." The movie star didn't sound particularly sad.

He leaned his hand on the door jamb. "You got the lights fixed in there, ma'am?"

"Yes. Go away."

Fine by him. Just hearing her voice made his heart speed up a tick, and he didn't like it. He'd turned away and put his hat back on when he heard the door open.

"Wait. Do you know anything about refrigerators?"

He glanced back and did a double take. She was standing there with a dish towel on her head, its blue and white cotton covering her face. "What in the Sam Hill are you—"

"I don't want you to see me. Can you fix a refrigerator?"

"Probably." He took his hat off as he stepped back under the awning, but she didn't back up to let him in. "Can you see through that thing?"

She held up a hand to stop him, but her palm wasn't quite directed his way. "Wait. Do you have a camera?"

"No."

"How about a cell phone?"

"Of course."

"Set it on the ground, right here." She pointed at her feet. "No pictures."

He fought for patience. This woman was out of her mind with her dish towel and her demands. He had a horse to stable for the night and eight more to feed before he could go home and scarf down something himself. "Do you want me to look at your fridge or not?"

"No one sets foot in this house with a cell phone. No one gets photos of me for free. If you don't like it, too bad. You'll just have to leave."

Travis put his hat back on his head and left. He didn't take to being told what to do with his personal property. He'd crossed the flagstone and stepped onto the hard-packed dirt path to the barn when she called after him.

"That's it? You're really leaving?"

He took his time turning around. She'd come out to the edge of the porch, and was holding up the towel just far enough to peek out from under it. He clenched his jaw against the sight of her bare stomach framed by that tight black clothing. She hadn't gotten that outfit at any Western-wear-and-feed store. The thigh-high boots were gone. Instead, she was all legs. Long, bare legs.

Damn it. He was already hungry for food. He didn't need to be hungry for anything else.

"That's it," he said, and turned back to the barn.

"Wait. Okay, I'll make an exception, but just this one time. You have to keep your phone in your pocket when you're around me."

He kept walking.

"Don't leave me. Just…don't leave. Please."

He shouldn't have looked back, but he did. There was something a little bit lost about her stance, something just unsure enough in the way she lifted that towel off one eye that made him pause. The way she was tracking him reminded him of a fox that had gotten tangled in a fence and wasn't sure if she should bite him or let him free her.

Cursing himself every step of the way, he returned to the porch and slammed the heel of his boot in the cast iron boot jack that had a permanent place by the door.

"What are you doing?" Her head was bowed under the towel as she watched him step out of one boot, then the other.

"You're worried about the wrong thing. The cell phone isn't a problem. A man coming from a barn into your house with his boots on? That could be a problem. Mrs. Mac-Dowell wouldn't allow it." And then, because he remembered the sister's distress over the extremes to which the paparazzi had apparently gone in the past, he dropped his cell phone in one boot. "There. Now take that towel off your head."

He brushed past her and walked into the kitchen, hanging his hat on one of the hooks by the door. He opened the fridge, but the appliance clearly was dead. "You already checked the fuse, I take it."

"Yes."

Of course she had. That had been why the lights had gone on and off.

She walked up to him with her hands full of plastic triangles. "These wedges were in the doors. I took them out because I thought maybe you had to shut the door all the way to make it run. I don't see any kind of on-off switch."

The towel was gone. She was, quite simply, the most beautiful woman he'd ever seen. Her hair was messed up from the towel and her famously blue eyes were puffy from crying, but by God, she was absolutely beautiful. His heart must have stopped for a moment, because he felt the hard thud in his chest when it kick-started back to life.

She suddenly threw the plastic onto the tile floor, making a great clatter. "Don't stare at me. So, I've been crying. Big deal. Tell all your friends. 'Hey, you should see Sophia Jackson when she cries. She looks like hell.' Go get your phone and take a picture. I swear, I don't care. All I want is for that refrigerator to work. If you're just going to stand there and stare at me, then get the hell out of my house."

If Travis had learned anything from a lifetime around animals, it was that only one creature at a time had better be riled up. If his horse got spooked, he had to be calm. If a cow got protective of her calf, then it was up to him not to give her a reason to lower her head and charge. He figured if a movie star was freaked out about her appearance, then he had to not give a damn about it.

He didn't, not really. She looked like what she looked like, which was beautiful, red nose and tear stains and all. There were a lot of beautiful things in his world, like horses. Sunsets. He appreciated Sophia's beauty, but he hadn't intended to make a fuss over it. If he'd been staring at her, it had been no different than taking an extra moment to look at the sky on a particularly colorful evening.

He crossed his arms over his chest and leaned against the counter. "Is the fridge plugged into the wall?"

She'd clearly expected him to say something else. It took her a beat to snap her mouth shut. "I thought of that, but I can't see behind it, and the stupid thing is too big for me to move. I'm stuck. I've just been stuck here all day, watching all my food melt." Her upper lip quivered a little, vulnerable.

He thought about kissing just her upper lip, one precise placement of his lips on hers, to steady her. He pushed the thought away. "Did you try to move it?"

"What?"

"Did you try to move it? Or did you just look at it and decide you couldn't?" He nodded his head toward the fridge, a mammoth side-by-side for a family that had consisted almost entirely of hungry men. "Give it a shot."

"Is this how you get your jollies? You want to see if I'm stupid enough to try to move something that's ten times heavier than I am? Blondes are dumb, right? This is your test to see if I'm a real blonde. Men always want to know if I'm a real blonde. Well, guess what? I am." She grabbed the handles of the open doors and gave them a dramatic yank, heaving all her weight backward in the effort.

The fridge rolled toward her at least a foot, making her yelp in surprise. The shock on her face was priceless. Travis rubbed his jaw to keep from laughing.

She pressed her lips together and lifted her chin, and Travis had the distinct impression she was trying to keep herself from not going over the edge again.

That sobered him up. He recrossed his arms. "You can't see them, but a fridge this size has to have built-in casters. No one could move it otherwise. Not you. Not me. Not both of us together."

"I didn't know."

"Now you do."

She seemed rooted to her spot, facing the fridge. With her puffy eyes and tear-streaked face, she had definitely had a bad day. Her problems might seem trivial to him—who cared if someone snapped a photo of a famous person?—but they weighed on her.

He shoved himself to his tired feet. "Come on, I'll help you plug it in."

"No, I'll do it." She started tugging, and once she'd pulled the behemoth out another foot, she boosted herself onto the counter, gracefully athletic. Kneeling on Mrs. MacDowell's blue-tiled counter, she bent down to reach behind the fridge and grope for the cord. Travis knew he shouldn't stare, but hell, her head was behind the fridge. The dip of her lower back and the curve of her thigh didn't know they were being fully appreciated.

When she got the fridge plugged in, it obediently and immediately hummed to life. She jumped down from the countertop, landing silently, as sure of her balance as a cat. He caught a flash of her determination along with a flash of her bare skin.

Hunger ate at him, made him impatient. He picked his hat up from its hook by the door. "Good night, then."

"Where are you going?"

"Back to work." He shut the door behind himself. Stomped into the first boot, but his own balance felt off. He had to hop a bit to catch himself. He needed to get some food and some sleep, then he'd be fine.

The door swung open, but he caught it before it knocked him over. "What now?"

"I need groceries."

There was a beat of silence. Did she expect him to magically produce groceries?

"Everything melted." She looked mournfully over her shoulder at the sink, then back at him, and just...waited.

It amazed him how city folk sometimes needed to be told how the world ran. "Guess you'll be headed into town tomorrow, then."

"Me? I can't go to a grocery store."

"You need a truck? The white pickup is for general use. The keys are in the barn, on the hook by the tack room. Help yourself."

"To a truck?" She literally recoiled a half step back into the house.

"I don't know how else you intend to get to the grocery store. Just head toward Austin. Closest store is about twenty miles in, on your right."

"You have to get the groceries for me."

"Nope. It's May." He stuck his hat on, so his hands were free to pick up his second boot and shake the cell phone out of it.

"It's May? What kind of answer is that? Do you fast in May or do a colon cleanse or something?"

He looked up at her joke, but his grin died before it started. Judging by the look on her face, she wasn't joking. "The River Mack rounds up in May."

She looked at him, waiting. He realized a woman from Hollywood probably had no idea what that meant.

"We're busy. We're branding. We have to keep an eye on the late calving, the bulls—"

He stopped himself. He wasn't going to explain the rest. Managing a herd was a constant, complex operation. Bulls had to be separated from cows. The cow-calf pairs had to be moved to the richest pastures so the mamas could keep their weight up while they nursed their calves. Cows who had failed to get pregnant were culled from the herd and replaced with better, more fertile cattle.

Sophia flapped one hand toward the kitchen behind her. "I have nothing to eat. You have to help me."

He stomped into his second boot. "Not unless you're a pregnant cow."

At her gasp, he did chuckle. "Or a horse. Or a dog. You could be a chicken, and I would have to help you. I keep every beast on this ranch fed, but you, ma'am, are not a beast. You're a grown woman who can take care of herself, and you're not my problem."

She looked absolutely stricken. Had he been so harsh?

"Listen, if I'm going toward town, I don't mind picking you up a gallon of milk. That's just common courtesy. I expect you to do the same for me."

"But I can't leave the ranch."

"Neither can I." He touched the brim of his hat in farewell. "Now if you'll excuse me, I've got horses to feed before I can feed myself."

Chapter Four

A pregnant cow.

It was fair to say women pretty much spent their lives trying not to look like pregnant cows. Yet if Sophia Jackson, Golden Globe winner and Academy Award nominee, wanted help on this ranch, she needed to look like that cow she'd hugged in the middle of the road.

She didn't look like that. She looked like a movie star, and that meant she would get no help. No sympathy.

That was nothing new. Movie stars were expected to be rolling in dough and to have an easy life. Everyone assumed movie stars were millionaires, but she was more of a hundred-thousandaire. Certainly comfortable and a far cry from her days pointing at mattresses with a smile, but the money went out at an alarming rate between jobs. Even when she was not being paid, Sophia paid everyone else: publicists, managers, agents, fitness trainers, fashion stylists…and her personal assistant, Grace.

Sophia had to pay them to do their jobs, so that she could land another job and get another burst of money. An actor only felt secure if the next job got lined up before the current job stopped paying. Then, of course, the next job after that needed to be won, a contract signed, and more money dished out.

There would be no new jobs, not for nine months. Sophia slid her palm over her perfectly flat, perfectly toned abs. The whole pregnancy concept didn't seem real. It was a plus sign on a plastic stick and nothing more. She didn't feel different. She didn't look different.

Alex the Stupid Doctor had explained that she was only weeks along, and that for a first-time mother, especially one who stayed in the kind of physical shape the world expected Sophia to be in, the pregnancy might not show until the fourth or fifth month. Maybe longer.

She could have filmed another movie in that time...

But nobody in Hollywood wanted to work with her...

Because she'd fallen for a loser who'd killed her hardworking reputation.

Round and round we go.

Always the same thoughts, always turning in that same vicious cycle.

If only she hadn't met DJ Deezee, that jerk...

She picked up the goose salt shaker and clenched it tightly in her fist. For the next nine months, instead of paying her entourage's salaries, Sophia would be paying rent on this house. The rent was cheaper than the stable of people it took to sustain fame, which was fortunate, because the money coming in was going to slow considerably. Her only income would be residuals from DVD sales of movies that had already sold most of what they would ever sell—and her old manager and her old agent would still take their cut from that, even though they'd abandoned her.

She was going to hide on this ranch and watch her money dwindle as she sank into obscurity. Then she'd have to start over, scrambling for any scrap Hollywood would throw to her, auditioning for any female role. Her life would be an endless circle of checking in with grouchy temps, setting her head shot on their rickety card tables, taking her place in line with the other actors, praying this audition would be the one. She wasn't sure she could withstand years of rejection for a second time.

She shouldn't have to. She'd paid her dues.

The ceramic goose in her hand should have crumbled from the force of her grip, the way it would have if she'd been in a movie. But no—for that to happen, a prop master had to construct the shaker out of glazed sugar, something a real person could actually break. Movies had to be faked.

This was all too real. She couldn't crush porcelain. She could throw it, though. Deezee regularly trashed hotel rooms, and she had to admit that it had felt therapeutic for a moment when he'd dared her to throw a vase in a presidential suite. Afterward, though…the broken shards had stayed stuck in the carpet while management tallied up the bill.

She stared for a moment longer at the goose in her hand, its blank stare unchanging as it awaited its fate. "There's nothing we can do about any of this, is there?"

The kitchen was suddenly too small, too close. Sophia walked quickly into the living room. It was bigger, more modern. Wood floors, nice upholstery, a flat-screen TV. A vase. The ceilings were high, white with dark beams. She felt suddenly small, standing in this great room in a house built to hold a big family. She was one little person dwarfed by thousands of square feet of ranch house.

She heard her sister's voice. Her mother's voice. *You've got nowhere else to go. You cannot live with me.*

She couldn't, could she? Her sister was in love, planning a wedding, giddy about living with her new husband. There was no room for a third wheel that would spin notoriety and paparazzi into their normal lives.

And her mother... Sophia could not move back home to live with her. Never again. Not in this life. Other twenty-nine-year-olds might have their parents as a safety net, but Sophia's safety net had been cut away on a highway ten years ago.

The ceilings were too high. The nausea was rising to fill the empty space, and it had nothing to do with pregnancy, nothing at all. Sophia squeezed her eyes shut and buried her face in her clenched fists. The little beak of the salt shaker goose pressed into her forehead, into her hard skull.

The house was too big. She got out, jerking open the front door and escaping onto the wide front porch. In the daylight, the white columns had framed unending stretch of brown and green earth. At night, the blackness was overwhelming, like being on a spaceship, surrounded by nothing but night sky. There were too many stars. No city lights drowned them out. She was too far from Hollywood, the only place she needed to be. *All alone, all alone...*

This was not what she wanted, not what she'd ever wanted. She'd worked so hard, but it was all coming to nothing. Life as she'd known it would end here, on a porch in the middle of nowhere, a slow, nine-month death. Already, she'd ceased to exist.

She hurled the salt shaker into the night, aiming at the stars, the too-plentiful stars.

The salt shaker disappeared in the dark. Sophia's gesture of defiance had no effect on the world at all.

I do exist. I'm Sophia Jackson, damn it.

If she didn't want to be on this ranch, then she didn't have to be.

You know how to drive, don't you? Turn the car around, then, instead of blowing that damned horn.

There was a truck, the cowboy had said. A white truck. Keys in the barn. She ran down the steps, but they ended on a gravel path, and her feet were bare. She was forced off the path, forced to slow down as she skirted the house, crossing dirt and grass toward the barn.

I don't want to slow down. If I get off the roller coaster of Hollywood, I'll never be able to speed back up again. I refuse to slow down.

She stepped on a rock and hissed at the pain, but she would not be denied. Instead of being more careful, she broke into a sprint—and stepped on an even sharper rock. She gasped, she hopped on one foot, she cursed.

I'm being a drama queen.

She was. Oh, God, she really was a drama queen—and it was going to get her nowhere. The truck would be sitting there whether she got to the barn in five seconds or five minutes. And then what? She'd drive the truck barefoot into Austin and do what, exactly?

I'm so stupid.

No one had witnessed her stupidity, but that hardly eased her sense of embarrassment as she made her way more carefully toward the barn. It was hard to shake that feeling of being watched after years of conditioning. Ten years, to be precise, beginning with her little sister watching her with big eyes once it was only the two of them, alone in their dead parents' house. *But Sophie, do you know how to make Mom's recipe?*

Don't you worry. It will be a piece of cake.

Sophia knew Grace had been counting on her last remaining family member not to crack under the pressure of becoming a single parent to her younger sister. Later, managers and directors had counted on Sophia, too, judging whether or not she would crack before offering her money for her next role. She'd had them all convinced she was a safe bet, but for the past five months, the paparazzi had been watching her with Deezee, counting on her to crack into a million pieces before their cameras, so they could sell the photos.

The paparazzi had guessed right. She'd finally cracked. The photos were all over the internet. Now no one was counting on her. Grace didn't need her anymore. Alex had stuck Sophia in this ranch house, supposedly so she'd have a place where no one would watch her. Out of habit, though, she looked over her shoulder as she reached the barn, keeping her chin up and looking unconcerned in the flattering light of the last rays of sunset. There was no one around, only the white pickup parked to the side. The cowboy must have gone to get his dinner.

Well, that made one of them. Sophia realized the nausea had subsided and hunger pangs had taken its place. Maybe inside the barn there would be some pregnant-cow food she could eat. She slid open the barn door and walked inside.

Not cows. Horses.

Sophia paused at the end of the long center aisle. One by one, horses hung their heads over their stall doors and stared at her.

"You can quit staring at me," she said, but the horses took their time checking her out with their big brown eyes, twitching their ears here and there. The palette of their warm colors as they hung their heads over their iron and wood stalls would have made a lovely setting for a rustic movie.

There were no cameras here, no press, no producers. Sophia stopped holding her breath and let herself sag against the stall to her right. Her shoulders slumped under the full weight of her fatigue.

The horse swung its head a little closer to her, and gave her slumped shoulder a nudge.

"Oh, hello." Sophia had only known one horse in her life, the one that the stunt team had assigned her to sit upon during a few scenes before her pioneer character's dramatic death. She'd liked that horse, though, and had enjoyed its company more than that of the insulting, unstable director.

"Aren't you pretty?" Sophia tentatively ran the backs of her knuckles over the horse's neck, feeling the strength of its awesome muscles under the soft coat. She walked to the next stall, grateful for the cool concrete on the battered soles of her feet.

The next horse didn't back away from her, either. Sophia petted it carefully, then more confidently when the horse didn't seem to mind. She smoothed her hand over the massive cheek. "Yes, you're very pretty. You really are."

She worked her way down the aisle, petting each one, brown and spotted, black and white. They were all so peaceful, interested in her and yet not excited by her. Except, perhaps, the last one with the dark brown face and jet-black mane. That horse was excited to snuffle her soft nose right into Sophia's hair, making Sophia smile at the tickle.

"It's my shampoo. Ridiculously expensive, but Jean Paul gives it to me for free as long as I tell everyone that I use it. So if he asks, do a girl a favor and tell him you heard I use his shampoo."

How was that going to work, now that she was out of the public eye? She rested her forehead against the horse's solid neck. "At least, he used to give it to me for free."

The horse chuffed into her hair.

"I'd share it with you, but I might not get any more, actually. Sorry about that, pretty girl. Before this is all over, I may have to borrow your shampoo. I hear horse shampoo can be great for people's hair. Would you mind?"

"Did you need something else?"

Sophia whirled around. Mr. Don't-or-Else stood there, all denim and boots and loose stance, but his brown eyes were narrowed on her like she was some kind of rattlesnake who'd slithered in to his domain.

"I thought you were gone," she said. She adjusted her posture. She was being watched after all. She should have known better than to drop her guard.

"You are not allowed in the barn without boots on."

The horse snuffled some more of her hair, clearly approving of her even if her owner didn't. "What's this horse's name?"

"No bare feet in the barn." The cowboy indicated the door with a jerk of his strong chin—his very strong chin, which fit his square jaw. A lighting director couldn't ask for better angles to illuminate. The camera would love him.

Travis Chalmers. He'd tipped his hat to her this afternoon as he'd sat on his horse. Her heart had tripped a little then. It tripped a little now.

She'd already brought her ankles together and bent one knee, so very casually, she set one hand on her hip. It made her body look its best. The public always checked out her body, her clothing, her makeup, her hair. God forbid anything failed to meet their movie star expectations. They'd rip her apart on every social media platform.

Travis had already seen her looking her worst, but if he hoped she'd crack into more pieces, he was in for a disappointment.

Sophia shook her hair back, knowing it would shine even in the low light of the barn. "What's the horse's name? She and I have the same taste in shampoo."

"He's a gelding, not a girl. You can't come into the barn without boots or shoes. It's not safe. Is that clear?"

Sophia rolled her eyes in a playful way, as if she were

lighthearted tonight. "If it's a boy horse, then what's *his* name? He likes me."

The cowboy scoffed at that. "You seem to think all of my stock like you."

"They do. All of them except you."

Travis's expression didn't change, not one bit, even though she'd tossed off her line with the perfect combination of sassy confidence and pretty pout. He simply wasn't impressed.

It hurt. He was the only person out here, her only possible defense against being swallowed by the loneliness, and yet he was the one person on earth who didn't seem thrilled to meet a celebrity.

Supposedly. He was still watching her.

The audition wasn't over. She could still win him over.

The anxiety to do so was familiar. Survival in Hollywood depended on winning people over. She'd had to win over every casting director who'd judged her, who'd watched her as impassively as this cowboy did while she tried to be enchanting. Indifference had to be overcome, or she wouldn't get the job and she couldn't pay the bills.

With the anxiety came the adrenaline that had helped her survive. She needed to win over Travis Chalmers, or she'd have no one to talk to at all. Ever.

So she smiled, and she took a step closer.

His eyes narrowed a fraction as his gaze dropped down her bare legs. She felt another little thrill of adrenaline. This would be easy.

"You're bleeding," he said.

"I'm—" She tilted her head but kept her smile in place. "What?"

But he was impatient, walking past her to glare at the floor behind her. "What did you cut yourself on?"

She turned around to see little round, red smears where

she'd stopped to greet each horse. "It must have been a rock outside. I stepped on a couple of rocks pretty hard."

"Good."

"Good?"

He glanced at her and had the grace to look the tiniest bit embarrassed. "Good that it wasn't anything sharp in the barn. If it had been a nail or something that had cut you, then it could cut a horse, too."

"Thanks for your concern." She said it with a smile and a little shake of her chandelier earrings. "Nice to know the horses are more valuable than I am."

"Like I said earlier, it's my job to take care of every beast on this ranch. You're not a beast. You should know to wear shoes."

She wasn't sure how to answer that. She couldn't exactly insist she *was* a valuable beast that needed taken care of, and she certainly wasn't going to admit she'd run outside in a panic. Actors who panicked didn't get hired.

"Come on. I'll get you something for the bleeding."

He walked away. Just turned his back on her and walked away. Again.

After a moment, she followed, but she hadn't taken two steps when he told her to stop. "Don't keep bleeding on the floor."

"What do you want me to do?" She put both hands on her hips and faced him squarely. Who cared if it didn't show off her figure? She'd lost this audition already.

"Can't you hop on one foot?"

This had to be a test, another trick to see if she was a dumb blonde. But Travis turned into a side room that was the size of another stall, one fitted out with a deep utility sink and kitchen-style cabinets.

He wasn't watching her to see what she'd do, so maybe it wasn't a joke. After a moment of indecision, she started hopping on her good foot. The cut one hurt, anyway, and it was only a few hops to reach the sink.

Travis opened one of the cabinets. It looked like a pharmacy inside, stocked with extra-large pill bottles. He got out a box of bandages, the adhesive kind that came in individual paper wrappers. The kind her mother had put on her scrapes and cuts when she was little.

I am not going to cry in front of this man. Not ever again.

He tapped the counter by the sink. "Hop up. Wash your foot off in the sink."

"Why don't you come here and give me a little boost?"

He stilled, with good reason. She'd said it with a purr, an unmistakably sexual invitation for him to put his hands on her.

She hadn't meant to. It had just popped out that way, her way to distance herself from the nostalgia. Maybe a way to gain some control over him. He was giving her commands, but she could get him to obey a sexual command of her own if she really turned on the charm.

Whatever had made her say that, she had to brave it out now. Sultry was better than sad. Anything was better than sad.

She tossed her hair back, her earrings jingling like a belly dancer's costume. She turned so that she was slightly sideways to him, her bustline a curvy contrast to her flat stomach.

"The counter's too high for me. Give me a hand…or two."

Come and touch me. Her invitation sounded welcoming. She realized it was. He was nothing like the sleek actors or the crazy DJs she'd known, but apparently, *rugged outdoorsman* appealed to her in a big way. *You've got a big green light here, Mr. Cowboy.*

"Too high for you," he repeated, without a flicker of sexual awareness in his voice. Instead, he sounded impatient as he cut through her helpless-damsel act. "I already watched you hop up on Mrs. MacDowell's counter tonight."

Of course the counter height had been a flimsy excuse; it had been an invitation. She refused to blush at having it rejected. Instead, she backed up to the counter and braced her hands behind herself, letting her crop top ride high. With the kind of slow control that would have made her personal yoga instructor beam with approval, she used biceps and triceps and abs, and lifted herself slowly onto the counter with a smooth flex of her toned body. People would pay money to see a certain junior officer do that in a faraway galaxy.

Travis Chalmers made a lousy audience. He only turned on the water and handed her a bar of soap.

She worked the bar into a lather as she pouted. Even Deezee wouldn't have passed up the chance to touch her. Actually, that was all Deezee had ever wanted to do: touch her. If it wasn't going to end in sex, he wasn't into it. She'd texted him ten times more often than he'd texted her between dates. His idea of a date had meant they'd go somewhere to party in the public eye or drink among VIPs for a couple of hours before they went to bed together. There'd been no hanging out for the sake of spending time together.

Sophia held her foot still as the water rinsed off the suds. She'd mistaken sex for friendship, hadn't she?

"It's not a deep cut. You should heal pretty quickly." Travis dabbed the sole of her foot dry with a wad of clean paper towels, which he then handed to her. Before she could ask what she was supposed to do with damp paper towels, he'd torn the paper wrapper off a bandage and placed it over the cut. He pressed the adhesive firmly into her skin with his thumb. There was nothing sexual in his touch, but it wasn't unkind. It was almost…paternal.

"Do you have kids?" she asked.

For once, he paused at something she'd said. "No."

You ought to. There was something about his unruffled, unhurried manner…

Dear God, she wasn't going to start missing her father, too. She couldn't think about parents and sister any longer. Not tonight.

She snatched her foot away and jumped lightly off the counter, landing on the foot that hadn't been cut. She held up the wad of damp towels. "Where's the trash?"

"You need those paper towels to wipe up the blood on your way out. I'll get you something to wear on your feet."

On her way out. She was dismissed, and she had to go back to the empty house in the middle of nowhere. She didn't want Travis to fetch her boots; she wanted him to carry her. He was a man who rode horseback all day. A cowboy who stood tall, with broad shoulders and strong hands. He could carry her weight, and God knew Sophia was tired of carrying everything herself.

She wanted his arms around her.

But she'd failed this audition. He wasn't interested in her when she was either bossy or cute. He wasn't fazed by her sultry tone, and he didn't care about her hard-earned, perfect body. He wasn't impressed with her in any way.

She gingerly stepped into the center aisle to see where he'd gone. Across from the medical room was another stall-sized space where it seemed saddles got parked on wooden sawhorses. The next room was enclosed with proper walls and a door, with a big glass window in the wall that looked into the rest of the barn. She could see a desk and book-case and all the usual stuff for an office inside. She felt so dumb; she hadn't known barns had offices and medical clinics inside.

Travis came in from the door at the far end of the aisle from the door she'd used. He dropped a pair of utilitarian rubber rain boots at her feet. "These will get you back to the house. Return them tomorrow, before sundown."

"So specific. Bossy much?" She could hear the snotty teenager in her voice. Whatever. She hated feeling dumb.

"Whoever brings the horses in tomorrow might want to wear them when they hose down a horse, so have them back by then."

It was a patient explanation, but she hated that he could tell she didn't know squat about how a ranch was run. "Someone else is coming? You're not going to be here tomorrow night?"

"We take turns during roundup. One of the other hands will have a chance to come in and shower and sleep in a bed. Someone's usually here before sundown."

"But I can't let anyone else see me."

He shrugged. "Then don't come into the barn at sundown."

Then turn the car around. Then go to the grocery store. As if life were that simple.

"If you do come into the barn, wear boots. Dish towels are optional. Good night." He walked back into the medical stall, closing cabinet doors and shutting off the light.

Dish towels are optional. The man thought she was a big joke. With as much dignity as she'd once been forced to muster each time a casting director had said *Don't call us, we'll call you*, Sophia stepped into the galoshes and headed for the door, bending over to wipe up little red circles as she went.

Travis returned to the center aisle in time to watch the most beautiful woman in the world stomp out of his barn like a goddess in galoshes. She slid the barn door closed behind herself with what he was certain was a deliberate bang.

Samson, his favorite gelding and apparent lover of women's shampoo, kept his head toward the door, ears pointed toward the spot where the woman had disappeared. Travis realized he and the horse were both motionless for a moment too long.

"You can stop staring at the door. She's not coming back."

The horse shifted, stamping his foot.

"All right, damn it, you're right. Her hair smelled amazing. Don't get used to it. We've got work tomorrow. It'd take more than a pretty woman to change our ways."

Chapter Five

Three days, he stayed away.

The days were easy, filled with dirt and lassos as the animals were rounded up, counted, doctored. Calves bawled for their mamas until the cowboys released them and let them run back to the waiting herd. Travis had to change his mount every few hours to give the horses a rest, so the additional challenge of controlling different mounts with their unique personalities kept his attention focused where it ought to be.

But for three nights…

He'd stretch out on his bedroll and stare at the stars while thinking of one in particular, the star that had fallen onto his ranch. Insomnia wasn't a problem after a day of physical work, but when his tired body forced his mind to shut down, he continued thinking about Sophia Jackson in his sleep. Sophia got flirty, she got angry, she was strong and she was weak, but she was always, always tempting in every dream version of her that his brain could concoct. For three nights, he dreamed of nothing else.

It was damned annoying.

In the afternoon of the fourth day, he rode in with Clay Cooper, the hand who was next up for a night off. As foreman, Travis had to get to his office to keep up with the never-ending paperwork that went with running any business. That was reason enough for him to leave camp for the night. Not one cowboy was surprised when he left with Clay and the string of horses that were due for a day's rest and extra oats in the barn.

But Travis knew the real reason he was going in was to check on the famous Sophia Jackson. He was tired of fighting that nagging feeling that he needed to keep an eye on her, a feeling that hadn't gone away since the moment he'd met her in the road.

The house came into view. Travis's horse perked up. Travis had worked with horses too long for him not to understand what drove their behavior. The horse had perked up with anticipation because the rider had perked up with anticipation.

Travis rolled his shoulders. Took off his hat and smacked the dust off his thigh. Relaxed into the saddle.

There was nothing to anticipate. He was going to see Sophia Jackson soon. No big deal. Sophia was a movie star, but he wasn't starstruck.

The horse walked on while Travis turned that thought over once or twice. It felt true. Sure, he'd seen her in *Space Maze*. It would be hard to find someone who hadn't seen that movie. But from the tantrum she'd thrown about being stared at, and from her sister's fear of the paparazzi, he didn't think the Hollywood lifestyle was very attractive. It would have been better if she hadn't been a movie star.

Better for what?

Just easier all around. He put his hat on his head and turned back to check the string of horses following Clay. All was well.

As the foreman, he was riding in to check on the new person renting the MacDowells' house, same as he'd check on any new cowboy who came to the ranch. Hell, he'd check on any new filly or fence post. Once he was sure the MacDowells' guest had gotten her groceries and her fridge was still running, he'd mentally cross her off his to-do list and move on to the next item: he needed to order more barb wire before they got down to the last spool.

He and Clay rode past the house. Travis had planned to help Clay put up the horses first at the bunkhouse's stable before checking on Sophia, but he noticed that Clay didn't even toss a glance toward the house. It hit Travis that none of the hands who'd come and gone from camp seemed to be aware anyone was living in Mrs. MacDowell's house. Travis would've told them there was a guest staying there. No big deal. But no one had mentioned seeing any signs of life for the past three nights.

There were no signs of life now. No lights on. No curtains open to take in the evening sunset. No rocking chair on the porch out of place. Sophia was keeping herself hidden pretty well, then. Or…

Or Sophia Jackson had left the River Mack ranch.

I don't want to be here, anyway, she'd said, hand poised over the car's steering wheel.

It was the most likely explanation. He'd wanted her to leave when he'd first met her, so he ought to be relieved. Instead, that nagging need to see her intensified. He had to know if she was still on his land or not.

"I'll see you tomorrow," he said to Clay. He let his horse feel his hurry to reach Mrs. MacDowell's kitchen door until he stopped her at the edge of the flagstone patio.

There, stretched out on one of the wooden picnic tables, was Sophia. She was laid out like she was the meal, her clothing white like a tablecloth, her body delectable, but her eyes were closed and her hand was open and relaxed as she slept.

He dismounted and looped the horse's reins loosely around the old hitching post. His horse tossed her head with a jangle of tack and the heels of Travis's boots made a hard noise with each step as he crossed the flagstone, but Sophia remained fast asleep.

He ought to be thinking of Sleeping Beauty, he supposed. Sophia was as beautiful as a princess in her innocent white clothing, if a princess wore shorts and a shirt.

Instead, he couldn't get the idea of a feast out of his head. Here was a woman who'd be a banquet for the senses. Old college memories came back, Humanities 101 and its dry textbook descriptions of Roman emperors who'd held feasts where the sex was part of the meal. The image of a fairy tale princess battled briefly with the Roman feast, but Travis's body clearly clamored for Rome.

He stopped at her side. Looked down at her, but didn't touch. "Sophia."

She didn't stir. He said her name again and waited, wondering how a shirt and shorts could look so sexy. Finally, he shook her arm. "Sophia, wake up. It's Travis."

She jerked awake, then jerked away from him, like an animal instinctively afraid of attack.

Fanciful notions from college studies evaporated in an instant. "Whoa. It's just me."

She rolled off the table, off the far side, so that she stood with the table between them. It was a seriously skittish move.

"What are you doing here?" she asked.

"This is my ranch."

"Ha. You don't spend a lot of time on it." She pushed her hair back with both hands, pausing to squeeze her temples with her palms as she looked around the horizon. "Crap. Is it already sunset?"

"Clay's already taken the horses to the stable."

She looked toward the barn, alarmed. "Did this Clay guy see me?"

Travis didn't envy her Hollywood life at all. She seemed to be on edge all the time.

She wasn't wearing a shirt and shorts, after all. It was all one piece, almost like a child's pajamas. Maybe she was embarrassed to be caught outside in her pajamas. "Don't worry. You're looking at the barn, not what we call the stables around here. The stables are on the far side of the horse pasture. You can't see it from the house."

He paused. He didn't have a reason to tell her more, except that it might buy her some time to ease into being awake. "The stables are close to the bunkhouse. Cowboys living there keep their horses in the stables."

But judging by the way she rubbed the sleep from her eyes, she'd tuned him out after *Clay can't see you*. "I have to go inside. It's sunset."

"No one else is due in tonight." His words fell on deaf ears. Sophia stepped up on the little porch and disappeared into the house.

Travis caught himself staring at the closed door like Samson had the other night. He cursed under his breath and went to untie his horse. He had his answer: Sophia Jackson was still here. She looked fine, better than fine. She looked healthy as all get-out. It was time to move on and order that barb wire.

He led his horse to the barn. Caring for the mare was a familiar routine, one that should have let him unwind, but he had to work to ignore a lingering uneasiness. He unsaddled the mare, stored the tack, then took her outside to rinse the sweat marks from her coat with a garden hose.

The galoshes were sitting neatly by the hose, pushing his thoughts right back to Sophia.

Her presence in the barn that night had been unsettling in general. So had been one of her questions in particular: *Do you have kids?*

For just for a second, he'd thought he'd like to be able to answer *yes*. He was thirty-one and settled. He'd stood there with Sophia Jackson's perfectly arched foot in his hand and pictured himself married with a couple of little ones that he'd have to keep out of trouble. *It would be good to be a dad*, he'd thought for that flash of a second.

In reality, he didn't see himself getting married, and in his world, having children meant being married. He had nothing against the institution; he could understand why men did marry. Many a rancher's wife provided dinner every evening and clothes mended with love. They baked cakes and grew tomatoes in the garden, like Mrs. MacDowell.

Or there were wives who were partners in handling cattle. Travis hired the same husband and wife team every fall when it came time to move the cattle to auction. The two of them seemed happy roping and riding together, and they worked smoothly in sync.

But Travis was fine as a bachelor. He liked his own cooking well enough. Working alone never bothered him. He was where he wanted to be, doing what he wanted to do. In order to even consider upending a perfectly good life, he'd have to meet a woman who was damned near irresistible.

Like Sophia Jackson.

Not anything like her. He'd need to find a woman who

was irresistible but not crazy enough to wear a dish towel on her head and spike-heeled boots on a dirt road.

Unless that's what makes her irresistible.

He turned the hose back on and stuck his head in the stream of water.

Listen to yourself. A rancher's wife and a movie star are two different creatures. Too different.

This woman slept on top of a picnic table in the middle of the day. Crazy. A man did not marry *crazy*. A man didn't want *crazy* to be the mother of his children. Irresistible had nothing to do with it.

He shook the water out of his too-long hair as he unbuttoned his sweat-soaked plaid shirt and peeled it off. He had to lean over pretty far to keep the water off his jeans and boots, but the hose was good for taking off the first layer of trail dirt from his arms and chest.

Feeling a hundred times more clearheaded, he shut off the water and turned the mare loose in the paddock. His office was inside the barn. He kept a stack of clean T-shirts there. While he was at his desk, he'd order a dozen spools of quality barb wire, so he wouldn't have to give it a second thought for the rest of the year. Barb wire would be ordered—check. The MacDowells' houseguest was doing fine—check. He'd move on to the next item on his list.

He shoved the galoshes aside with the edge of his boot and left the darkening sky before the stars could come out and taunt his resolve.

It was useless. As he strode into the barn, he heard a distinctively feminine gasp. In the twilight of the barn's interior, Sophia practically glowed, all silver-blond hair and short, white pajamas. A star, right here in his barn. There was no list; there was nothing else to think about.

She dropped her gaze first.

Slowly.

She took him in deliberately, her gaze roaming over his wet skin, from his left shoulder to his right. To his bare chest. Lower.

I'm not the only one around here who's hungry, then.

The knowledge blinded him for a moment. To hell with the kind of woman he ought to want. Sophia was the woman he *did* want. Full stop. And he wanted her badly.

She came a step closer.

As water drops rolled down his skin, blood pounded through his veins, his desire for her ferocious in a way that was unfamiliar, as if he'd never really wanted a woman before.

She was about to say something, but as her lips parted, her gaze flicked from his chest back up to his eyes. Whatever she saw in his expression made her own eyes open wider. Whatever she'd been about to say turned into a little whoosh of "oh."

He couldn't remember feeling this power before, not for any of the women who'd been so likely to be right for him. After dating for weeks or months or, once, a whole year, none had turned out to be right after all. Yet Sophia had only to exhale an *oh*, and the years of friends and lovers blurred into nothing. This woman was the one he'd been starving for.

Hunger caused problems on a ranch. Stallions kicked out stalls. Bulls destroyed fences.

"Why are you here?" he demanded. *Why you? Why now?*

She took a step closer, and a part of him—too much of him—didn't give a damn about the answers to his own questions. He just wanted her to keep coming.

She hesitated.

Then she took that next step closer, but it was too late. Her split-second pause, the widening of her eyes by a fraction of an inch, had betrayed the tiniest little bit of...fear? Perhaps fear of this power between them. Perhaps fear of him, personally. He was the bigger one, the stronger one, the one with an admittedly fresh surge of testosterone coursing through his body.

But he was no animal, no common beast, just as he'd told her she wasn't. He knew what was in his heart and mind and soul, and she didn't need to fear him.

She couldn't know that yet, not for certain. They barely knew one another. Travis didn't have any kind of minimum time limit in mind for how long he ought to know a woman before taking her to bed, but he did know this: she had to be one-hundred-percent certain of what she wanted. Sophia Jackson did not know what she wanted.

Travis stepped back.

Her frown of confusion was fleeting, replaced by a new look of determination. She sauntered up to him, nice and close. Then she looked down his body again, her feminine eyelashes shading her blue eyes, turning him on as she ran one fingertip over his damp forearm.

"I came out here because it's lonely in that house. Very lonely."

God, that purr of hers...

It was an act. She was a good actress, but he'd seen that moment of fear or uncertainty or whatever it had been. Hunger couldn't be ignored forever, but it wouldn't kill a man to wait. Travis didn't intend to act on it or even talk about it in his barn just because he'd been caught out half-naked by a woman in skimpy pajamas.

He balled up his plaid shirt and used it to wipe the water off one arm, then the other. He pitched it through his open office door to land on his chair. *No feast today, Princess.*

"Did you need something before I go home?" he asked.

Her sexy act flipped to a more authentic anger pretty

quickly. Apparently, she didn't take rejection well. "I don't need anything from you. I didn't even want you to be here. I came to see the horses."

"Is that so? In your pajamas and bare feet?" He turned his back on her and went into his office. He grabbed a T-shirt off the stack he kept on a bookcase. When he turned back, he nearly plowed her over; she'd followed him into his office, all indignation.

"I'm wearing sandals, and these aren't pajamas. You wish you could see me in my pajamas. You wish."

Her attempt at a set down was so childish, it sounded almost cute. Travis had to hide his smile by pulling his T-shirt over his head. No harm in letting her think she'd scored a point against him.

"This is a *romper*," she huffed. "Straight from the runway. By a designer in Milan whom I wouldn't expect you to know. My stylist snatched it right out from under Kim K's nose. She probably died when I wore it first."

He stood with his hands on his hips, looking down at her, wondering what a guy like him was supposed to do with a girl like her. "I don't know Kim, but it looks real nice on you."

"Yeah. Sure." Apparently, she didn't believe his compliment. She turned her back on him and left the office, her designer clothes all in a white flutter.

Travis scrubbed his face with both hands. Then he shut off the lights and left the office, closing the door firmly. The barb wire could wait until tomorrow.

Sophia was nuzzling the spotted nose of a nice Appaloosa Travis had borrowed from the neighboring ranch for roundup. Travis watched her for a minute. The horse was loving the attention. *You're getting more action than I am, buddy.*

Still, Travis had to appreciate a person who had a natural affinity for horses. Her talent had to be natural and not learned, because he didn't think Sophia had ever set foot in a barn in her life before this week. She was wearing flip-flops, for crying out loud.

"Where's my horse?" she asked, keeping her eyes on the Appaloosa.

"Your horse?" He didn't like her wording. She had no idea what it meant to own a horse. To train, to groom, to feed, to care for without fail, to rely on when there was nobody for miles around.

"The boy horse whose name you won't tell me. You left, and you took him with you. You took all of them. I came out here to say hello to the horses, and they were gone. Every single one."

Damn if she didn't sound like she was going to burst into tears.

"They aren't pets. They work."

"I returned the galoshes, just like you wanted, but you took the horses away. Without those horses, I've got no one to talk to. You're not interested in talking to me...or doing anything else with me."

Travis was good at picking up on animal behavior, not a woman's, but he could read her well enough. She felt betrayed. Lonely. Hell, she'd curled up into a ball and cried on a kitchen floor just days ago.

He'd have no peace of mind until he figured her out.

"Okay. You want to talk? Let's talk."

Chapter Six

The cowboy wanted to talk.

Sophia wasn't sure if he was kidding. She combed her fingers through the spotted horse's mane and peeked at big, bad Travis Chalmers. He looked pretty serious. Then again, that was his default expression. He grinned a little now and then, but otherwise, he was a serious guy.

Not a guy. A man.

A serious man who walked around here like he ran the place. Which she supposed he did, but still…

Travis took some kind of rope-and-leather thing that was hanging over an empty stall door and coiled it up. Tied it off. Tossed it into the room where the saddles were. It landed in a crate. It seemed that being in charge meant keeping everything in order.

Deezee would have dumped the crate out, flipped it upside down, and stood on it like it was his stage, whooping and hollering and making sure no one else could talk while he was around.

Travis glanced down the row of stalls to the neat stack of perfectly square hay bales, then leaned back against a support post and gave her his full attention. Apparently nothing else was out of place—except her. "What did you want to talk about?"

She wasn't about to unburden herself to this man. She could pour out her regrets to the horses tomorrow morning. She didn't want Travis to know what an idiot she'd been. What an idiot she'd thrown away her career for.

Yet she'd just complained that she didn't have anyone to talk to, and Travis had called her on it. She had to come up with something to say. "What's this horse's name?"

Travis dipped his chin toward the horse, as matter-of-fact as if her question wasn't childish. "That's Arizona. He was named for the state. Texas isn't really known for Appaloosas. He was bought in Arizona as a wedding gift."

Oh, no. Please don't be married.

Dumb reaction. The man looked hot when he was shirtless. So what? That didn't mean she wanted to have a relationship with him. It didn't matter if he was married or not. Still...

"Not a gift for your wedding?" She tried to sound unconcerned.

"Trey Waterson's wedding. His brother gave him the horse. They own the ranch just west of us."

But Travis had that little bit of a grin about his mouth; he knew exactly why she'd asked. Her acting skills must be getting rusty already. She wished she hadn't run her finger down that muscled forearm, chasing a water droplet. She wished she hadn't made that stupid comment about being lonely.

She wished he hadn't rejected her.

"I'm not married," he said, making things perfectly clear. "Never been."

The horse, Arizona, shook his mane like Sophia wanted to. *That's right, horse. We don't care, do we?*

"So you don't own these horses, then. You're just the babysitter." She sneered the word *babysitter*.

She wished it back as soon as she said it. It was so rude. When had she started responding to everything as if she needed to insult someone before they could insult her?

But the answer was easy: when she'd spent too much time with Deezee and his buddies. Their ribbing and one-upmanship had been constant. At first, it had been a novelty to be treated like one of the guys instead of a flawless movie star, but she'd soon figured out that if she gave them an inch, they took a mile.

So maybe I've thrown up a few walls to protect myself. That's normal.

"Some horses are mine. Some are the ranch's." Travis patted Arizona's spotted neck. "Some I borrow."

His voice was so even. He couldn't care less about her nasty little dig. Did nothing irritate him? Or did he just not show it?

Judging by Travis Chalmers, it seemed the great actors in the movie industry, legends like Clint Eastwood and John Wayne, had acted their cowboy roles with more accuracy than Sophia had realized. They delivered their dialogue in an almost monotone way—never too excited, never shouting. Like Travis. Nothing like Deezee.

It was hard to imagine Travis jumping from a church pew to a communion railing and yelling *Yo, where's the ho?*

Deezee had meant her. Sophia had been standing in the vestibule of the Caribbean chapel, trying not to sweat through her white dress, waiting for the church music to start so she could walk down the center aisle to promise her life to him. He'd meant it as a joke, just another outrageous zinger for his posse's amusement. He hadn't bothered to change into a clean T-shirt. It was just a spontaneous elopement. No need to go to any trouble.

No crying in front of the cowboy.

"What's my horse's name?" she demanded. "And where is he?"

"Samson. He's still at camp. And he's my horse, not yours."

"Why did you ride that other horse today, then, if Samson belongs to you?"

"Because that other horse is mine, too. I own four right now, but you could say I babysit the rest."

Thank goodness the man's only facial expressions were somber and barely-a-grin. She'd insinuated that he owned nothing. If he laughed at her for how far she'd missed the mark, she might go all crazy diva on him. She couldn't stand to be laughed at.

"Four? For one man?" But her sarcasm was stupid, and she knew it.

"You can't ride just one horse all day, every day during roundup. That's why Arizona comes to work with me during roundup, see? So I have more horses to rotate. But Samson, he's a real special cow horse. I save him for when I'm actually cutting cattle out of the herd. It's a waste of talent to use him just to ride in from camp."

"You sound like a coach with a sports team."

"I hadn't thought of it that way. It's like setting up your batting order in baseball, now that you mention it. Samson's my star player. Don't tell Arizona that, though. He's been doing a great job pinch-hitting all week." Travis winked at Sophia, and he smiled. Not a grin, but a real smile that reached all the way to his eyes, a smile like she was in on the joke and part of his team.

Good Lord. The man was beautiful. She'd thought he

looked hot the moment she'd spotted him riding toward her that first day on the road. Kind of stern and remote, but so masculine on horseback that he'd cut through her haze of misery. Today, shirtless and dripping wet, he'd looked like an athlete, a man in his prime, serious and strong. But when he smiled—oh, why would the women of Texas keep a man like this out here in the middle of nowhere?

For once in her life, she was the one doing the staring.

"B-baseball?" she repeated. Then, because she'd stuttered, she sneered a little, just to let him know she didn't care. "What would a cowboy know about baseball? There aren't enough humans around here to get a game going."

She caught the slightest shake of his head as he crossed his arms over his chest—a move that did lovely things to stretch that T-shirt tight around his biceps. His smile lingered. He found her amusing. Damn him.

"True enough. This cowboy played shortstop in college. Was there anything else you wanted to talk about besides horse names and baseball?"

She wondered how much of her thoughts he could guess. Could he see how much she wished she hadn't ruined her chances with a guy like him by making a huge mistake with a guy like Deezee?

You're an actor, Sophia. Don't let him see anything.

It was easier just to alienate people so they'd leave her alone. Her bridges were already burned. To hell with it.

"College? For a cowboy? What do they teach you, not to step in horse manure?"

Finally, *finally*, she'd pricked through his infuriatingly calm exterior. His eyes narrowed as she held his gaze defiantly.

That's right, I am a rattlesnake. You don't want to mess with me. She didn't want any man to mess with her, ever again.

His voice remained even. "My degree is in animal sciences from Texas A&M. They expect students to be smart enough to avoid horse manure before they enroll." He looked at her flip-flops, pointedly, and she fought the urge to curl her toes out of sight. "But I guess some people never do figure out what boots are for."

"Are you going to kick me out of your barn again?"

Please. Put me out of my misery. I'm screwing everything up here. Send me back to that awful, empty house and let me fall apart.

"I'm not your babysitter. You do what you want. If you don't have the common sense to stay out of trouble, well, some folks have to learn the hard way."

"I think I can avoid cow patties, thank you very much. I have eyes."

Travis pushed away from the post. "Then you might want to get going. It's getting dark real quick. It'll be harder to see those cow patties, and critters that like to bite toes will start coming out, too. Those flip-flops aren't going to protect you from a snake or a rat."

A rat. She glanced around the aisle. This place was too neat and organized for rats.

"We keep a barn cat," Travis said, reading the skepticism she hadn't bothered to hide. "She's a good mouser, but she does earn her keep."

He wasn't going to kick her out. She was going to have to force herself back to the lonely house. She acted like it didn't freak her out. "I'm leaving, anyway."

"I'll walk you to the door."

She jerked her arm out of his reach and stepped sideways, the side of her foot hitting a square hay bale. It felt like hitting a porcupine, except for her toes. Her toes made contact with something furry.

"A rat!" She nearly knocked Travis over, jumping away from the hay bale.

He caught her with a hand on her arm, but he was already frowning at the floor, bending down and reaching—

"Don't touch it." She tried to yank him away from the rat. He stood up with something brown in his hand and she let go of his arm. "Ew."

"It's not 'ew.' It's a kitten."

It wasn't moving. For the first time since Travis had woken Sophia from her nap, she felt the nausea rising. "Did I—do you think I... I didn't hurt it, did I?"

She felt him looking at her, but she had eyes only for the kitten, the tiniest one she'd ever seen. Travis pressed its baby paws with his thumb, wiggling each limb as he did. "Nothing seems to be broken or bent. You didn't hurt it."

Thank goodness. She sank weakly onto the hay bale, then leaped up as the hay poked her rear right through her designer romper from Milan.

Travis didn't seem to notice. His attention was on the kitten. He pulled at the collar of his T-shirt and tucked the brown fluff in, keeping it in place with one hand.

"Shouldn't we put it back so the mother cat will be able to find it?"

"He's cold. The mother cat must have abandoned him a while ago. If I can get him warmed up, we might be able to slip him back in with his brothers, but this is the second time the mother has moved him out of her nest."

"Why would she do that?"

Travis shrugged, the kitten completely hidden by his hand. "She might sense that there's something wrong with it."

"But you said it's not hurt."

"As far as I can see. The mother might know something

I don't. Or the mother might have decided two kittens are all she can handle, so the third one gets abandoned."

"She leaves it out to die? That's awful. Can't you do something about that?" Anxiety tinged her voice, but she didn't care. Her anxiety to *not* see a kitten die felt pretty intense.

"I am doing something about that," he said drily. "I've got a kitten stuck down my shirt."

"You're going to keep it?" That sounded good. Really good.

He sat on the hay bale, the heavy denim of his jeans so much more practical than her white silk. "This kitten is really young. His eyes aren't open yet. His best bet for survival is with his mother."

Her anxiety spiked right back up. "But he has a terrible mother. She left him, just left the pitiful thing all alone. He's better off without her."

"No, he isn't." Travis spoke firmly, but he was looking at her with…concern. It took her a moment to recognize concern on a man's face. For the past ten years, the only person who'd ever looked at her with concern had been Grace. Her sister was the only one who'd ever cared.

Nausea tried to get her attention, but Sophia pushed it away. She didn't want to acknowledge it or what it might mean.

"You've never had a cat before, have you?" Travis asked.

"Ages ago, but she was neutered. You should neuter your cats. You have to neuter this one's mother right away. She's a bad mother. She doesn't deserve to have any more babies." Sophia pressed the back of her hand against her mouth abruptly to conquer the nausea.

But it was too late. The thing she didn't want to think about was now at the forefront of her mind: the little plus sign on that stick. Motherhood. Babies.

The word *pregnant* might not seem real to her, but Grace and Alex had been so deadly serious about it. They'd sat her down at Alex's kitchen table to talk through the options.

Sophia had immediately pounced on giving the baby up for adoption. It sounded simple. There'd be this baby that she would never even have to see, really, and the adoption agency would find the perfect couple. The couple would be happy. The baby would be happy. No harm all around.

That pregnancy test had probably been wrong, anyway, but adoption was a simple solution for a simple equation: one unwanted baby plus one couple who wanted a baby equaled success. Sophia would be doing a good deed. End of family meeting.

"Sophia." There was a definite note of concern in Travis's voice now, to match the way he was looking at her. "She might not be a bad mother. Sometimes Mother Nature knows more than we do. But for what it's worth, I agree with you about having cats neutered. This kitten's mother found us a couple of weeks ago. She moved herself in and was already pregnant. Accidents happen."

Oh god, oh god, oh god...

Tonight, faced with a few ounces of fluff she'd almost stepped on, Sophia suddenly realized what she'd left out of the equation: herself. Doing a good deed? She was the failure in the equation, not the hero. She was giving the baby away because she knew, deep down, she would be a terrible mother. She'd tried so hard with Grace, but she'd failed. Grace didn't even want to live with her anymore.

Travis had said the cat might have decided she couldn't handle that baby. Sophia knew she couldn't handle a baby, either. So what did that make Sophia? A terrible, horrible, selfish cat.

Travis tucked his chin into his collar and spread his fingers out, trying to see the kitten. "He's moving around. That's a good sign."

Sophia backed away from him, scared of the little bit of brown fluff and all that it represented.

"I'm going to go now." Her voice sounded thin, too high. "Good luck with the kitten."

She turned tail and ran. And ran. As fast as she could in the stupid flip-flops, she ran so that she was out of breath when she got back to the house.

It helped. It was only a sprint, maybe the length of a football field, nothing like the miles she'd had to put in to prepare for battling monsters in *Space Maze*, but she felt a little more normal. She felt her lungs and ribs expanding, contracting, taking in extra air. Muscles she hadn't used in weeks were suddenly awake, alive. She smoothed her hand over her stomach. The nausea was gone, and she felt hungry.

What she didn't feel was pregnant. Not one bit.

The pregnancy test's instructions had cautioned over and over that the results were not always accurate. Really, all that had happened was that Sophia had skipped a period, which was an easy thing to do. She probably wasn't even pregnant.

She was here to hide from the paparazzi, that was all. Her sister and Alex had both told Travis that. Sophia would lie low here for a few more weeks and let the media turn its attention elsewhere. Once they began a feeding frenzy on some other celebrity couple, Sophia would fly back to LA and start hunting for a new agent.

And you should make an appointment to get your tubes tied, because now you know you wouldn't be happy if you really were pregnant, and you'd be a lousy mother who couldn't take care of a baby, anyway.

She glanced out the kitchen window toward the barn,

where some knocked-up stray cat was apparently her spirit animal. If the kitten-killing cat had been sent to show Sophia how much she was lacking, she'd done her job tonight. It was a good thing Sophia was planning on letting someone adopt the baby, because she wouldn't be a good mother. It was a crushing revelation.

The only light on in the whole house was the little one over the stove. That was plenty. The boxes of nonperishable food were still lined up on the kitchen counter, and Sophia had spent the week working her way through them, left to right. She didn't need a lot of light to pour herself another bowl of organic raisins and bran flakes.

She sat at the table and poked at the dry cereal with her spoon for a while. The organic milk substitute had gotten warm that first day, so she'd dumped it down the drain. Without a housekeeper, a personal shopper, or a sister, it hadn't been replenished yet.

Sophia didn't care. She just wanted to sleep, even after the nap she hadn't meant to take outside today. That had been a stupid slip up. It would have blown her cover if anyone except Travis had come by.

She couldn't get her act together enough to do a simple thing like hide. She'd dared to go outside because the house felt too empty. The sun had felt good on her skin after four days indoors, so she'd stretched out and fallen asleep.

No surprise there. She'd been tired for years. She'd been looking for a break when she'd taken Grace for that vacation in Telluride, but five months of Deezee hadn't been very refreshing. She was more tired than ever now.

Except when she talked to Travis. She'd felt alive and awake when Travis had walked into that barn with no shirt on. Nothing like a half-naked, incredibly buff man to snap a girl out of a fog.

The expression in his eyes had taken her breath away.

Boy meets girl. Boy wants girl. Or rather, man wants woman. Woman had wanted him right back, with an intensity that she couldn't handle.

No surprise there, either. She couldn't handle anything in her life. But she'd felt like she was really alive for the first time in ages, so she'd been determined to see how far he would go.

Not very far. One touch with her finger, and he'd literally stepped back from her and put on a shirt. So much for her bankable box office sex appeal. She'd lost her career, her sister—and her ability to attract a man. She sucked. Her life sucked.

On that note, she left her bowl on the table, stumbled into the living room, and did a face plant on the sofa. She never wanted to wake up again.

Chapter Seven

"Sophia, wake up."

She jerked awake, heart pounding.

"It's just me. Travis. Are you okay?"

She sat up on the couch and dropped her face in her hands, willing her heart to slow down. She hated to be startled awake, because her first instinct was to flail about in case Deezee and his crew were in the middle of pulling some prank, like drawing on her face with a Sharpie just before she was expected to make an appearance. *It's funny, baby, whatchu getting upset for?*

She'd had to cancel that appearance, disappointing fans and angering her manager.

"I'm not okay. You just scared me to death, shaking my arm like that."

"Sorry. Nothing else was waking you up."

She was waking up now, fully aware of where she was and who was standing over her. "What are you doing here?"

"Checking on you."

"What are you doing in my house? Did you just open the door and walk in?"

"Yes."

"What are you, some kind of stalker?"

"No."

His implacable, even tone set her teeth on edge. "But you just walked into someone else's house. You don't see anything wrong with that, do you?"

"I knocked first." His cell phone was in his hand, but he slipped it into his back pocket.

She stood up, furious. "I deserve privacy. I rented this house. I get that you're all Mr. I-Run-This-Place, but the house is mine for the duration. You can't just walk in any time you please. Have you been spying on me while I was sleeping? Standing over my bed without me knowing it every night?"

"Of course not. Quit spooking yourself."

"Spooking myself? What does that mean? That's not even a thing."

"You're letting your imagination run away with you. I walked in just now because we don't tend to stand on ceremony out here in the country. We can't. If someone's in trouble, you have to help. You can call nine-one-one, but it can take a long time for help to arrive. We take care of each other."

The man sounded like he actually believed what he was saying. He was oblivious to the invasion of her privacy. Living in the country couldn't be that different than living in the city.

"You had no reason to think I was in trouble."

"I thought I'd come and tell you some good news, but it looked like nobody was home."

"So?"

"If you hadn't come back to the house, then where were you? You ran out of the barn like a bat out of hell, so I figured you'd made it back to your place in a couple of minutes, but it didn't look like you were here. You'd run somewhere else. It's full dark out there. You aren't wearing much, and a person can start to lose body heat pretty quick once the sun goes down. You only had on flip-flops. If you'd gotten hurt—"

"I was right here on my own couch, minding my own business."

"Good. Now I don't have to saddle up Arizona and go out to look for you."

You would have done that for me? But the calm way he was looking at her, the steadiness of his voice told the truth. Just the fact that it had even occurred to him to go looking for someone who might be missing was…

It made her feel kind of protected. A nice feeling.

Crap. It was hard to stay mad at a man who'd honestly been worried about her. Not just worried, either. He actually would have done something about it.

She crossed her arms over her chest, but she couldn't force any real sting into her voice. "Well, we need to have an understanding that you won't sneak into my house again. Where I'm from, that's called breaking and entering. It creeps me out. Even the paparazzi don't dare to walk in my door. Don't do it, okay?"

He took his time thinking about his answer. "All right."

"I mean it." She didn't need any man mounting horseback search parties for her sake. She didn't.

"This wasn't sneaking in," he said. "You have my word I never will. But if I think you're in trouble, I'm going to do whatever it takes to help you, whether you like it or not."

Sophia blinked. *Why, you bossy son of a*— But then she

realized she was looking at his back because he'd left the living room to go into the kitchen. She hurried after him.

He had already turned on the lights in the kitchen. He picked up her dry bowl of cereal. "Is this all you ate today?"

She stopped cold. There was only one reason a man would ask about that. Only one reason. "The paparazzi got to you already, didn't they?"

His gaze narrowed again.

I'm not the rattlesnake, dude. You are.

"I want to see your cell phone." She was seething. "How long have you been in here, photographing Sophia Jackson's hideout? Documenting Sophia Jackson's Hollywood diet secrets? Did you take pictures of me sleeping? Did you?"

"You're spooking yourself again."

"How much did they pay you? The kid at the deli by my condo got two thousand dollars for writing down my sandwich orders for a week. He took a photo of my sister picking up a bag with subs in it. When I didn't order a sandwich the next day, he lied and took a photo of someone else's sandwich. He got the cash. You know what I got?"

Travis set the bowl down with a soft curse.

He didn't want to hear her story? Too bad. He needed to know exactly what he was doing by giving the paparazzi supposedly harmless details of her life.

"I got reamed by America for setting a bad example for the youth of today. The youth of today! Because one of those youths took a picture of some insanely greasy concoction and claimed it was mine. Then everyone said the only way I could eat like that and keep my figure would be if I abused laxatives or stuck my fingers down my throat after every meal. The fact that they photographed me going in and out of a gym every single frigging day was irrelevant when it came to how I might be keeping my figure, but that's beside the point. I was suddenly personally responsible for every poor teenager with an eating disorder. I know how this game works, Travis. You'll get cash, and I'll get punished."

She nearly choked on his name. Travis—the betrayal shouldn't have hurt this badly. She didn't really know him any better than the deli counter kid.

"I'm not talking to any damned paparazzi. I don't think I've ever said that word out loud in my life. Paparazzi."

"I'm not stupid," she said, feeling very stupid for having let down her guard for an instant. "Since when does a big, tough cowboy suddenly take an interest in what kind of cereal a woman eats?"

"Since the big, tough cowboy got scared. Bad." He started walking toward her, two steps that covered most of the big kitchen. "I didn't just knock. I called the phone, too. You didn't move when I turned on the lights. I had my phone in my hand because I was going to call nine-one-one if I couldn't wake you. My grandpa had diabetes. I've seen what happens when a person's blood sugar gets too low. You scared me. That's all."

He took another step closer. She didn't back up, but she crossed her arms defensively. He was a lot of man, looming over her. A lot of man with a lot of honesty in his voice, and concern in his expression, and really beautiful brown eyes.

He ran his rough-warm palm over her arm, from her shoulder to her elbow, and kept his hand there, firm. "I'm very sorry I scared you in return."

Sophia felt her world turning. Pieces of her mind tumbled and landed in a new order. A better order. If she lived her life a different way…if she didn't always assume the worst…if she could believe someone wanted to help her instead of use her…

She could have a friend.

It was what she'd hoped for with Deezee. Things with him had started out with this kind of instant attraction, this desire to trust a man she barely knew.

Hope hurt.

Sophia took a step back.

Travis bowed his head, a quick nod to himself. When he looked up, he was the remote, stern foreman once more. "Do you always sleep so hard?"

He meant, *Is there something I should know about, because I'm responsible for all the horses and pregnant cows and cats around here?* She could hear it in his voice.

The truth would guarantee that he'd think of her as some kind of crazy diva: *No, I'm just sad. When I'm really sad, I deal with it by checking out of the world and going into hibernation.*

She couldn't tell him that.

"I'm just making up for a lack of sleep. A few years' worth of sleep."

"And do you always eat such a spartan diet? You never went to the grocery store, did you?"

"Don't start with that." This was why she didn't have friends. No one walked a mile in her shoes. No one understood.

She imitated his unruffled, even tone. "'If you need groceries, then go to the grocery store.' Everything is so easy for you, isn't it? You get to come and go as you please on any horse that strikes your fancy. You know what to do if you find a half-dead kitten, so you don't freak out. Of course you can decide whether or not you'll head to the store for more groceries."

She was afraid she might cry, but only because she wanted him to understand.

"Do you know why I have to wait for my sister to bring

me groceries? It's not because I'm a diva. It's because I'll get hurt if I go out by myself. It's happened before." She held out the arm he'd stroked. "See these little half moons? That's how much my fans love me. If I walk down a street, I'll let them take their selfies and then I'll try to say good-bye, and they'll dig their fingernails into me. 'No, wait. You have to wait until my friend shows up.'

"I have to smile. I can't pitch a fit or else I'm a bitch or a diva or a monster. I've been held hostage, forced to wait on a sidewalk for a stranger's friend while people start penning me in from every direction. The police will stop to see what the crowd is about and they'll smile and wave at me. So I just sign autographs until it's the policeman's turn, and then I have to smile while I ask them to keep people from hurting me. 'Gee, Officer, could you possibly escort me back to my hotel?'"

Oh, hell, her eyes were tearing up, but she didn't care. Deezee had gotten off on these stories. He'd wanted them to happen to him. But Travis was frowning, and she didn't know if it was because he believed her or if it was because he thought she was *spooking* herself again.

But she had more proof, a secret that only a few hair-stylists knew about. She turned her back to him and started pawing through her hair, piling her hair up until her fingertips found it, that dime-sized bit of her scalp where no hair grew. "This is how much they love me. Right after *Space Maze* came out, I was spotted at a grocery store. Honest to God, I had no idea how much people loved that movie. They pulled the hair out of my head as a souvenir. That's love. Right there."

She jabbed at the spot, such a small scar left after so much blood and pain, but Travis's hand stopped hers. He smoothed his thumb over the scar. She closed her eyes, remembering his thumb on the sole of her foot, smoothing an adhesive bandage into place, making everything better.

"I'm sorry," he said.

She dropped her hands, and her hair fell back into place with a shake of her head, just like Jean Paul had designed it to do. It was such a great perk of fame, those great haircuts and free shampoo. What a lucky girl she was.

"I'm sorry," Travis repeated, gruff words that whispered over her hair.

She felt all the fight go out of her. She couldn't remember what was supposed to take its place. Before Deezee, before the breakthrough roles, before her parents' deaths... what had life been like when she hadn't fought for everything?

She opened the door so Travis could leave, facing him with what she hoped was a neutral expression and not a desolate one. "You don't have to worry if you don't see me around. I think any normal person in my position would stay out of sight. It's just that my future brother-in-law told me that the MacDowells said I could trust the foreman, so I... I showed myself to you. Everyone else will just have to think there's a vampire living in the house or something."

Travis nodded and picked his hat up from the table. He must have tossed it there instead of using the hook by the door. It was the sort of thing someone might do in a rush.

He walked out the door. Sophia realized he already had his boots on. He'd come in without stopping at the boot jack, breaking his own rule about boots in the house. He'd really been worried about her.

A little rush of gratitude filled some of the empty space inside her.

"Travis?"

He turned back to her, his expression serious, illuminated

by the light from the kitchen. Beyond him, the night was black, the night he would have ridden in, looking for her.

"I'm not a crazy recluse. I'm just a recluse, okay?"

"I get it."

She'd been holding her breath. Now she could breathe.

He tapped his hat against his thigh. "I never told you the reason I came looking for you in the first place. That kitten got more lively when he warmed up, so I found the mother cat's new hiding spot. She didn't object when I slipped him in with his brothers."

"Oh." She took a deeper breath. The night air felt fresh. "Oh, that's great news. She's not a terrible mother after all."

"I never said she was. She had her reasons. We just don't know what they were. I put out some extra food, in case she was worried about having enough to eat. The other barn cat will probably get to it first, but it's worth a try. When I left, she was pretty relaxed and letting all three kittens nurse."

Maybe Sophia was crazy after all, because it felt like Travis had just given her the best gift. "Thank you. Thank you so much."

"I wouldn't want you to get too hopeful. That kitten's had a rough time of it so far."

"But now he'll be okay."

"We've given him a chance, at least. I'll see you when I get back in a few days. Good night." He touched the brim of his hat, and walked into the dark.

A few days?

She shut herself in the house.

Chapter Eight

She didn't wake up until noon.

What was the point? Everyone was gone again. Everyone meaning Travis and the horses.

Sophia was willing to bet that Travis had been saddling up those horses before dawn, true to the cowboy stereotype. She looked out the window toward the empty barn and tried not to feel resentful that the horses had been taken away. They had to work.

She wished she had to work. Resentment for her ex bubbled up, a toxic brew that made her stomach turn.

Thanks, Deezee.

Actually, Deezee was probably working, too. The more he partied, the more people wanted to pay him to appear at their parties. The more outrageous he got, the more bookings he got. Busting into that Texas Rescue ball and making a scene had been a smart thing for him to do. During their week in Saint Barth, his cell phone had blown up with offers.

Not hers.

A movie studio didn't make job offers to actors who skipped town without notice. A production couldn't build a PR campaign if their star said outrageous, unpredictable things. What helped Deezee's career killed hers.

Looking back, she doubted Deezee had realized how much he was hurting her. She doubted he would have cared if he had.

But she should have known better. She should have cared.

Deezee had lied to her. He'd cheated on her with other women. But he hadn't forced her to party like a rock star. That was her fault.

Thanks, Sophia.

She couldn't spend all day at the kitchen window, waiting to see which cowboy would come in at sundown. It wouldn't be Travis; that was all that mattered. She couldn't be seen by anyone else. She couldn't make another stupid mistake like she had yesterday, falling asleep on the picnic table. Alex and Grace wouldn't be able to pull another great hiding spot out of thin air. This was it. This was her only place to sleep, eat, hide and sleep some more.

But today, she didn't have the desire to go right back to sleep. She felt at least a little bit rested for a change. She'd slept in a real bed instead of crashing on the couch with the television on.

All week, she'd been avoiding the master bedroom. It was too spacious and too obviously someone else's room, with its family photos of little boys and a handsome father from decades past. She knew Mrs. MacDowell was a widow. She didn't like to look at photos of the dead father. She had her own.

But last night, after Travis had left, she'd wandered into one of the smaller bedrooms, one that looked like it was intended for guests. It had a queen-sized bed instead of a king. It had paintings of Texas bluebonnets on the walls instead of family photos. She'd been able to sleep there.

Great. So now she wasn't sleepy, but she still couldn't leave the house. Her one little foray to the picnic table yesterday had almost resulted in blowing her cover, because she'd lacked enough common sense to come back inside when sitting in the sun made her drowsy. She had no common sense. No self-discipline. She was in a prison of her own making, because she couldn't handle her own life.

Round and round her thoughts started to go. She hated them, because they always led to the same conclusion: she was a failure. She hated herself, and she was stuck.

But a new voice broke through the old soundtrack.

If you want to go outside, then open the door and walk outside.

Travis.

If he saw her standing here, if he could hear what she was saying to herself in her head, he would cut through all the nonsense with one of those infuriatingly simple solutions.

You're a grown woman, he'd say. A grown woman who was standing here, wishing she could go outside for a breath of fresh air but afraid that would be some catastrophic mistake. She'd fall asleep on a picnic table again, and let down Alex and Grace, and be laughed at in the press for being found on a cattle ranch, of all places. If she went outside, it would start a chain of disasters. It made sense to her.

Or it had, before last night. Before she'd spent some time with Travis and realized that all the puzzle pieces didn't have to go together in the complicated order she'd been putting them.

If you don't want to be in here, then open the door and go out there.

She opened the kitchen door, and stepped on a pile of zucchini.

She cursed as the zucchini scattered. She spewed every variation of the F-bomb that Deezee had ever shouted while playing a combat video game. She'd hated the way he'd lost control when he killed animated, imaginary enemies, yet she sounded just like him.

She shut up. It was zucchini, not the end of the world. Heck, her own *Space* character had managed to save an entire civilization without resorting to so much drama.

The zucchini rolled to a stop. A note was wedged into what remained of the pyramid by the door.

Sophia—
    When I got to my house, I saw that Clay had left a bunch of zucchini in my sink. His mother had a bumper crop, and she stopped by the bunkhouse when no one was there and left a ton in their kitchen. I don't think it's breaking and entering if someone's mother does it. The real crime here is that nobody can eat as much zucchini as Clay's mother grew. I'm passing off some of it onto you. It might make a nice change from cereal.
—Travis
P.S. I left you some milk in case you don't actually like your cereal dry. It's in the barn fridge. Please wear boots or shoes. You have enough scars. I don't want you to get any more.

Sophia stared at the letter. The man had been doing just fine, dropping little smart-aleck comments, but then he'd had to finish it up with that line about the scars. She must be crazy after all, because she felt all choked up by a hastily written P.S.

Sophia picked up the zucchini one by one, cradling them in her arm like a bouquet, and carried them into the kitchen. She put the zucchini in the sink. The letter she spread out on the counter. She read it again and smoothed out the crease. Read it again.

Then she went into the master bedroom, where Alex had left her suitcases. She hadn't unpacked them yet. Just reaching in and wearing the first thing she touched had taken all the energy she had, but now she lifted out the neat piles of clothes and carried them down the hall to the bluebonnet bedroom.

Trip after trip, she emptied the suitcases her sister had filled for her. As Sophia's personal assistant, Grace had been packing her bags ever since they'd moved to LA. Maybe Sophia hadn't wanted to unpack these final suitcases. Alex was going to be the person Grace took trips with from now on. These were the last shirts her sister would ever fold for her with care and love.

"This is depressing as hell." Sophia spoke the words loudly, but her voice didn't have to reach lofty rafters in here. The carpet and quilts of the guest bedroom absorbed the sound. The words weren't as scary out loud as they were when they echoed in her head.

Whether or not it was depressing, whether or not it was some kind of symbolic final vestige of her life with her sister, the suitcases had to be unpacked now, because Sophia needed her shoes. The only boots she had were the thigh-highs with the killer heels, but she knew that Grace would have packed workout clothes and a selection of running shoes for Sophia to choose from, depending on her mood and her clothes' color scheme.

She found the sneakers. Sophia left the empty suitcase

on the king-sized master bed. In her bedroom, she changed into a shirt that had sleeves and a pair of shorts that barely covered her rear but were made of denim. She laced up her most sturdy pair of cross-trainers and once more opened the kitchen door.

She wasn't going to fall asleep or get caught by a stranger or ruin her career. She was going to get some milk that Travis had left for her in the barn.

Nothing bad was going to happen.

The fresh air cleared the last bit of fog from Sophia's head as she walked the hundred yards or so to the barn.

The heat of the day was building. Her yoga instructor would say every molecule of hot air shimmered with energy that she could welcome into her lungs with intentional breaths. Sophia could practice here, doing yoga outside on the flagstone, holding poses that took all her concentration in the May heat. If she set an alarm clock tomorrow, she could get up a little earlier and go for a run before it got too hot.

If she really wanted more work in Hollywood, that would be the smart thing to do. Having a great body was an essential part of winning roles. If she let herself go too long without exercise, she'd pay a price. She really didn't want to keep paying for stupid decisions. *If you want to keep your fitness level, then work out.*

She'd have to be careful who saw her. But if only she and Travis were around, and he should happen to catch her in the middle of a workout in her painted-on exercise clothing…her muscles working, her skin glistening…

The possibilities sent a sizzle of sexual energy through her.

She slid open the barn door, using chest muscles that still felt strong despite weeks of laziness. Every LA personal trainer emphasized pectoral tone to keep the breasts high. Having good breasts was part of her job.

She'd only had to reveal them once in her career, during a love scene in a serious crime drama. Her male co-star's bare buttocks had been in the frame as well. As makeup artists had dabbed foundation on his butt cheeks and brushed shadow into her cleavage, the two of them had attempted awkward jokes until the director had called for quiet on the set. For hours, her costar kept popping some kind of bubblegum-flavored mints that smelled grossly sweeter with each take. There had been nothing sexy about filming that scene, but the director had known what he was doing, and the final cut had looked scorching hot on the big screen.

The movie had only gotten modest box office distribution, but Travis might have seen it. Had he found it arousing? He must have. One couldn't be human and not find the finished scene arousing.

She shut the door behind herself. The interior of the barn was dim after the blinding sun. She took a moment to let her eyes adjust, leaning against the same post Travis had leaned against last night. He'd given her his time and attention, willing to talk. Only to talk.

Not willing to be seduced. Not even by a movie star.

That sizzle died. When she'd reached out to touch him, he'd pulled on a shirt and left her standing in his office. Unemployed or not, she still looked like a movie star. What had she done that had made it so easy for him to resist her?

She walked slowly down the aisle, evaluating her posture and carriage, working on it as an actor. If she saw herself on film now, what kind of character traits would she be relaying to the audience?

She hadn't been very convincing in the role of seductress last night. She didn't believe she was still a movie star, so she wasn't acting like a movie star. That had to be the problem. Deezee's infidelity had shaken her confidence. The publicity had been humiliating, so now Sophia must be giving off some kind of insecure ex-girlfriend vibe.

Guys hated that. If she could turn back time to the person she'd been before Deezee, she would have Travis eating out of the palm of her hand. He'd be grateful if she chased a water droplet over his skin with the tip of her finger, because the sexy and smart Sophia Jackson would be the one doing the chasing, not the depressed and lonely creature she'd turned into. Travis couldn't resist a movie star.

Could he?

He already had. When they'd met on the road, she'd seen the precise moment on his face when he'd first realized who she was, but he hadn't exactly fallen all over himself to get her autograph. He'd told her to get behind the wheel and drive herself off his ranch, actually.

Don't call us; we'll call you.

She paused at his office window. There was nothing in that functional space that implied he was enchanted by Hollywood or its stars. For the first time in her life, it occurred to her that being a celebrity could be a disadvantage.

She'd just have to make him want her, anyway.

Men had wanted her long before she was famous. Really, that was why she'd become famous. People of both sexes had always noticed her. *Charisma*, Grace called it. An aura. Whatever it was, it was the reason Sophia had been put in films. The public might think movie stars were noticeable because they were already famous, but that wasn't how it worked. The charisma came first. They were noticed first. Stardom came second.

Where did Travis fit in?

The refrigerator was in the medical room. She headed for it while fretting over sex appeal and stardom, wondering if she could stand rejection from a cowboy any better than from a producer, and nearly stepped on the proof that everything she worried about, all of it, was insignificant.

At her feet, curled into a little ball in front of the fridge, was the kitten.

Sophia picked him up gingerly. It was humbling to hold a complete living being in her hand. He was still alive for now, but he couldn't survive on his own. The weight of his impending mortality should have been heavy. It seemed wrong that he was little more than a fluffy feather in her palm.

Travis had said the kitten was weak to start with, and Sophia knew next to nothing about kittens. She was going to lose this battle. It was a pattern she knew too well. Losing her sister, losing her lover, losing her career, failing auditions, failing to keep her scholarship...

Failing. She hated to fail.

She studied the newborn's face. "I'm not a very good mother, either, but I'm going to try, okay?"

Then she slipped the kitten inside her shirt.

Chapter Nine

Travis was not obsessed with Sophia Jackson.

He just couldn't stop thinking about her.

He'd left the milk in the fridge this morning with no intention of returning for the rest of the week, but as the morning had turned into afternoon, he'd already started convincing himself that he should head back to his office this evening. There were too many things on his to-do list that he hadn't touched last night.

He'd touched Sophia's scars instead.

Why had she let him into her personal life like that?

I'm not a crazy recluse.

She wanted to be understood, that much was clear to him. He just didn't know how much to read into the fact that she wanted *him* to understand her.

A pickup truck pulled up to the fencing they'd built for this year's roundup. Travis recognized the pickup as belonging to one of the MacDowell brothers who was coming to work these last few days of branding and doctoring. Travis was grateful for the distraction. He left the calf pen to greet Braden.

Braden MacDowell, like his brothers, was a physician in Austin. He'd taken over the reins at the hospital his father had founded, but he valued his family's ranching legacy as well, so it wasn't unusual to see him here. At least one MacDowell was sure to lend a hand during the busy months, if not all three brothers.

Travis respected the MacDowells. They visited their mama. They knew how to rope and ride. And they'd been wise enough to hire him.

Not to get too full of himself, but it said a lot that they'd asked him to keep the River Mack thriving as a cow-calf operation. They could've just rented the land out to a corporate operation that maintained its headquarters in another state. Travis wouldn't have stayed on the River Mack in that case. He preferred to work with a family that knew how to keep their saddles oiled and their guns greased, as the saying went.

"I just got away from the office," Braden said as Travis walked up to him and shook hands. "I trust there's still plenty of fun to be had?"

"Talk to me tomorrow about how fun it feels. You leave your necktie and briefcase at home?"

The ribbing was good-natured. Braden was in shape, but there was still a big difference between bench-pressing weights in a gym and hauling around a hundred-pound calf who didn't appreciate being picked up.

"I've got aspirin in the glove box." Braden dropped the tailgate and thumped an oversized cooler. "I brought supplies."

Travis helped him carry the cooler full of sports drinks closer to the working crew and then helped himself to one.

He drank while Patch, one of the best cow dogs in Texas, greeted Braden.

They kept sports drinks in the barn fridge, too. When Sophia got the milk, she'd see them. Travis hoped she knew she was welcome to take whatever she needed. He should have told her that in the note, maybe, and damn it all to hell, he was thinking about her again. Would he go five minutes without thinking of her today?

"All right, back to work with you," Braden said to the dog, but to Travis's surprise, Braden didn't head for the work area himself. "How's Sophia Jackson treating my house?"

Travis forced himself to swallow his drink around the surprise of hearing her name spoken. She was a big secret he'd been keeping from everyone, but it made sense that Braden knew. Of course he knew; he must have signed the lease.

"The house looks the same as always. You can't tell there's anyone's living there."

"No sounds of breaking glass coming from inside? She hasn't set the couch on fire or gone rockstar and destroyed it yet?"

Travis frowned at the expectation that she might. The closest thing he'd seen to any wild behavior had been when Sophia had dropped the plastic wedges on the kitchen floor. No harm there. "I'm not one to spy on your house-guests, but there's been nothing like that."

She cries a lot. She sleeps a lot. Those insights were his. He didn't care to share them. It felt like it would be betraying Sophia. She didn't want to be stared at. She didn't want to be talked about. Fair enough.

"She's not my houseguest," Braden said, his tone tight. "She's my tenant."

Travis turned to look over the milling herd and the distant horizon, waiting.

Braden studied the horizon, too. "I was against renting the house to her, but one of the ER docs, Alex Gregory, is engaged to her sister. Alex seems to think she's salvageable. He offered to cosign the lease. If she destroys the place, he's good for it, but if my mother comes back from her year in Africa and finds her grandmother's antiques destroyed, money won't make it right."

Travis kept a sharp eye on the calm herd. There was no reason to believe they would suddenly stampede—but they could. "You got a reason for assuming she'd bust furniture?"

"You don't keep up with celebrity news," Braden said.

"I'm surprised you do." That was putting it mildly.

"Only when it affects me. Twice, Texas Rescue invited her to make an appearance to help raise awareness of their work. Twice, she blew their event. My wife and I were going to one of them. I was expecting this elegant actress. My wife was excited to meet her. Instead, this banshee ruined the ball before it even got started. I should have read the gossip earlier. She'd been trashing hotel rooms and blowing off events for months. Now she's living in my home. I don't like it."

It was incredible that MacDowell thought Sophia would destroy someone's family heirlooms, but Travis had known the MacDowells for the past six years. He'd known Sophia six days.

Travis killed the rest of his bottle in long, slow gulps. It took only twenty ounces for him to decide to trust his gut. Sophia didn't mean anyone any harm. He'd seen the physical evidence of the harm others had done to her, and he'd seen her crying her heart out when she thought she was alone. She was a woman who'd been pushed to the edge, but she wasn't going to destroy someone else's life-time of memories. She just wouldn't.

"She's serious about hiding," Travis repeated. "She's not going to do anything to attract attention to herself. Your stuff is safe."

Braden was silent for a moment. "She's beautiful, isn't she?"

Travis turned his head slowly, very slowly, and met the man's stare. "We weren't discussing Sophia's looks. If you think my judgment is so easily clouded, we'd best come to an understanding on that."

He and Braden gauged one another for a long moment, until, inexplicably, Braden started to grin. "I trust you on horses and I trust you on cattle. I've known you to have a sixth sense about the weather. Maybe you don't find women any harder to read than that, but as a married man, I'm not going to put any money down on that bet. It puts my mind at ease a bit to hear that you don't think Miss Jackson is going to fly off the handle, but I'm still going to stop by and pick up a few breakables before I go."

Travis saw his opportunity and took it. "She won't an-swer the door if she doesn't know you. I'll go in with you. I've got work at my desk I can knock out while you're gath-ering up your breakables. If we take the truck, we can be done and back here inside two hours."

"I'm locked out of my own house, technically." Braden sounded disgusted. "Landlords can't just walk into the property once it's been rented out."

Travis paced away from the kitchen door and Braden's legalities. The zucchini was gone. Sophia had gotten up and gone out, then. He wasn't going to jump to any crazy conclusions. She wasn't dead or dying, languishing some-where, needing his help.

Where was she?

There were no horses in the barn, or else that would have been the logical place to assume she was.

"Let's hit the barn," Braden suggested. "Maybe she'll show up while you're taking care of your paperwork."

Travis had barely slid open the barn door when he heard Sophia calling out.

"Hello? Is someone there? Can you help me?" The distress in her voice was obvious as she emerged from his office. He'd already started for her before her next words. "Travis! It's you. Thank God, it's you."

She started down the aisle toward him at a half run, clutching her heart with two hands.

They met halfway. He stopped her from crashing into him by catching her shoulders in his hands. At a glance, she didn't seem to be hurt. Her expression was panicked, but her color was normal and she seemed to be moving fine. "What's wrong?"

She peeled her hands away from her chest to show him. "It's the kitten. It's dying."

"It's the—" Her words sank in. Travis let go of her shoulders and turned away for a moment to control his reaction, a harsh mixture of relief and anger. He'd thought she was having a heart attack.

"Do you hear that?" she cried.

He turned to look, and yes, she was really crying. She dashed her cheek on her shoulder.

"His cries are just so pitiful. He's been pleading for help like that for six hours. I can't stand it. He cries until he's exhausted, and then he wakes up and cries again. I don't know what to do for him."

Her distress was real. She was just too softhearted for the hard reality that not every animal could be saved. Travis took off his hat and gestured with it toward the office. "Come on, I'll take a look. Did you say six hours?"

"I came in to get the milk from the fridge, and he was on the floor, just lying out there. I warmed him up like you did, but then I couldn't find the mother cat for the longest time. The kitten started crying while I went over every square inch of this place. It took me an hour to find her, but when I put the baby in with the others, the mother just up and left, like, 'Here, have three babies.'"

Travis pulled out his desk chair. "Have a seat."

"I've been in this chair all day. I couldn't look anything up on the internet about what to feed a kitten, because your computer is password protected."

"That it is."

She sat in the chair he offered, but she glared at him like he'd invented the concept of computer passwords just to annoy her. "You've got all these books on animals in here, but do you know what they contain? Info on how many calories are in a frigging *acre* of alfalfa to calculate how many calves it'll feed. Chart after chart on alfalfa and Bahia grass. What to feed a cow, how much to feed a cow, how much to *grow* to feed a cow. Who needs to know crap like that?"

"That would be me." Travis didn't dare smile when she was working through a mixture of tears and indignation. He let her vent.

"Do you know what those books don't contain? *What to feed a newborn kitten.* Not one word. I couldn't call you for help. You're out on a horse all day."

"I'll give you my cell phone number, but there's no reception out on the range. If you leave a message, it'll ping me if I happen to catch a signal."

Braden strolled into the office with a dish in his hand.

"Looks like you tried to give it a saucer of milk. On my mother's fine china."

Sophia jerked back in the chair, clutching the kitten to her chest.

Travis had seen that skittish reaction too many times. This time, he put his hand on her shoulder, a little weight to keep her from jumping out of her own skin.

"It's okay. This is Braden MacDowell, one of the ranch owners. He already knew you were here. Your name's already on his lease."

She sniffed and looked at Braden resentfully. "I remember you from that stupid ball. You're the CEO of the hospital."

"Guilty."

"You shouldn't sneak up like that. I thought I was alone with Travis. Usually only one person comes in at sundown."

The implication hit Travis squarely. "What if it hadn't been me tonight? You would've blown your cover. I told you it wouldn't be me tonight. You came out of that office without knowing who was here."

"Trust me, I had hours to think about that while this kitten cried his heart out. I knew whoever came in was going to get a big surprise, and then he was going to get rich. I'd have to pay him hush money to keep my secret. It's like being blackmailed, only you go ahead and get it over with and offer to pay them up front." She rested her head back on the chair and sighed. "It's only money. That's the way it goes."

Travis was stunned.

She frowned at him. "What did you expect me to do? I couldn't just let a kitten die because the paparazzi might find me."

"No, of course not." But of course, she could have done

exactly that. She could have left the kitten where a ranch hand might find it and then run away to hide in safety. But she'd stayed to comfort a struggling animal instead of leaving it to cry alone.

"Sorry I startled you," Braden said. "I'm surprised you remember me. We'd barely been introduced at the fundraiser when you…left."

"I remember everything about that night."

With that cryptic statement, she resumed her tale of frustration, how the kitten hadn't known what to do with the milk, and how she'd tried warming it and holding the kitten's mouth near the surface. Her story was full of mistakes, but it wasn't comical; she'd tried hard to succeed at something foreign to her.

He noticed something else as well. Now that Braden was present, her manner was slightly different. She sat a little straighter and told her story in a more measured way. The contrast was clear to Travis. When she'd thought it was just the two of them, she'd been more emotional. Raw. Real.

Sophia didn't keep her guard up around him. There was a trust between them, an intimacy that she didn't extend to everyone. He wondered if she was aware of it.

"I tried leaving the three kittens together. I snuck away and stayed away for at least half an hour. I wanted to give the mother a chance to come back for them, in case she was just scared of me, you know? But when I came back, they were all crying. All of them. The mother cat didn't come back until I took this kitten away again." Her blue eyes filled with tears, and she quickly turned away from Braden. She spoke softly to Travis. "For a while there, I thought I'd doomed them all."

"You were doing your best. You were being as kind as a person could be." And if he turned his back to Braden to shut him out of their private conversation, well, there was no crime in that.

The kitten began another round of plaintive, hungry mewing.

"The road to hell is paved with good intentions," she murmured. "Listening to this kitten cry has been hell."

"I imagine it has."

She looked up at him, tired and trusting. "I'm so glad you're here."

The words stretched between them, an imaginary line connecting just the two of them for one moment. Then it snapped. Her sleepy-lidded eyes flew open as she realized what she'd said. "To help, I mean. I'm so glad you're here to help."

She was still scared, then. Still unsure of this power between them. It made her nervous enough that she put up her guard, which for a movie star meant shaking back some incredible blond hair and flipping her tired expression to one filled with a devil-may-care bravado. "Besides, you just saved me a fortune in hush money."

Braden chuckled, the expected response, but Travis saw through the act. This wasn't a one-sided attraction on his part, but she wasn't ready to admit it. Now was not the time or place to do anything with the knowledge. He was a patient man. It was enough to know that she wanted to see him as much as he wanted to see her.

She still held the kitten in two hands against her chest, so Travis gave her a boost out of the chair by placing his hand under her elbow. "Come on. Abandoned kittens need a specific kitten milk replacer. Let's see if I have any around here. If I don't, Braden will go to the feed store and get you some."

Chapter Ten

The pickup rocked over the rolling terrain, sending the headlight beams bouncing off fence posts and mesquite trees. Although Braden drove with all the speed one could manage on rough roads, they were getting back to camp far later than Travis had expected. Travis was returning with a hell of a lot more baggage than he'd expected, too, and all of it was in his head.

Maybe in his heart.

Definitely in his body.

Damn it. Every time he thought checking on Sophia would set everything to rest, he got more than he bargained for.

They'd found some powdered milk replacer in the bunkhouse kitchen. There'd been just a few scoops leftover from some other cowboy's past attempt to help out another cat, so they'd taken it back to the barn. While Braden had made the run to the feed store, Travis had taught Sophia how to mix the replacer, how to slip an eyedropper into the kitten's mouth, how to hold the kitten a little counter-intuitively while feeding it.

There'd been physical contact between the two of them, and a lot of it. Shoulders and hips had brushed as they huddled over the kitten. Hands guided hands to find just the right angle or apply just the right amount of pressure. He'd cuffed up his sleeves, and the sensation of Sophia's soft skin on his exposed wrist or forearm ignited aware-ness everywhere. By the time the kitten had been settled into a small box with a bit of an old horse blanket, that in-cidental contact had become so addicting, neither of them had moved away.

Sophia had been nearly as relieved as the kitten when it fell asleep from a full belly instead of from exhaustion. It would have been the most natural move for Travis to drop a kiss on Sophia's lips. Not one of passion, but one of camaraderie, the kind between couples who'd been to-gether through thick and thin.

He'd almost kissed her. *You did well.*

She'd almost kissed him. *Thank you.*

But in the end, Braden had returned with enough milk replacer for ten cats, and Sophia had drifted closer to the light over the barn sink in order to read the instructions on the can. They said a kitten this young was going to wake up and cry for a feeding every two hours.

Travis was used to long nights caring for young or sick animals. Braden was a doctor who thought nothing of over-night shifts, but Sophia...

It turned out that movie production schedules pushed actors to work without sleep as well. Sophia didn't flinch at the schedule.

With his head, his heart, his body, Travis felt himself falling for her too deep, too fast.

Too reckless.

The pickup truck bounced out of the rut in the dirt road, and Travis cracked his head against the side window.

He cursed at an unapologetic Braden. "Your breakables would've been safer in the house. They probably just flew out of the truck bed."

Braden kept his eyes on the road. "I didn't take anything out of the house."

"You're not worried she's going to break everything?" Travis knew the past few hours had shown Braden a different Sophia Jackson than he'd been expecting to see, but Travis wanted to hear him say it. Anyone who maligned Sophia should have to eat his words.

"I've been thinking about that."

Not good enough. Travis managed a noncommittal grunt to keep him talking.

"I did see some pretty incriminating photos, but she was never alone while she was flipping birds and screaming at those photographers."

"Paparazzi," Travis corrected him. But hell, were there photos out there of beautiful Sophia being so ugly?

"That jerk of a boyfriend of hers is behind her in every one, or sometimes in front. Looked like he was shoving her out of his way in one. After seeing the way he crashed that ball, he probably was."

It was the last thing Travis wanted to hear. Not after all that warmth, all that soft skin, all those tears for a kitten. He couldn't let go of that. He couldn't let go of the Sophia he knew. He couldn't accept that she had a boyfriend.

"You got any more details than that?"

"It was a black-tie event. Thousand-dollar donation per ticket. Red carpet to give the guests a thrill for their money. You know how it is."

"Not really." *Get to the boyfriend.*

"Everyone's all pretty and on their best behavior. Every camera in the house is pointed at Sophia. That's what she's there for, to give everyone a little taste of glamor. People pay an outrageous price to eat dinner in the same room as the celebrities."

Had Sophia once enjoyed that?

Don't stare at me. Quit talking about me.

"Next thing I know, some jackass in basketball shoes and a ball cap is jumping on the table. Walking on the silverware, kicking the centerpiece, making a lot of noise. Alex pulled Sophia behind his back. That was the first thing I noticed, Alex keeping Sophia behind himself, so I knew this jerk had come to cause trouble for her."

There was nothing Travis could do about it but listen. His hand was clenched in a fist on his knee.

"My brothers and I were ready to take him out. He was standing on my wife's salad, goddammit, but once every camera in the place was focused on him, he dropped to one knee and started apologizing to Sophia. As apologies went, it was crap. Maybe a sentence. Alex was pissed. Her sister was stunned."

"And Sophia?"

Braden hesitated for only a moment. "She ditched her commitment to Texas Rescue and left with him. She looked pretty happy about it, so no one tried to stop her."

Travis couldn't speak. A knife in the chest would do that to a man. The thought of Sophia choosing to be with an ass who'd destroy the happiness of everyone around him was like a knife in the chest.

"But you see how that turned out. She's here alone. After getting to know her a little bit today, it's obvious the two of them aren't as alike as the photos make it look. My guess is that she's hiding from him as much as the rest of the world."

They hit another pothole, which gave Travis the perfect excuse to curse again. "I should have been told. Alex said she was hiding from cameras."

"If the boyfriend turns up again, things will break. More than my grandma's antiques. That kind of hyped-up guy dances too close to the line."

"Got a name?"

"DJ something. Something inane."

"*Paparazzi* is an inane word, too. I'll let the men know we're keeping everyone off the River Mack ranch whose name we don't already know."

"We would've been here sooner, but the gate at the main road was closed," Grace said.

Sophia nodded at her sister as if that made sense.

"All the gates were closed this time. I had to get out three times to open them. I saw a guy on a horse at the last one, the foreman we met last time. We waved at each other and he rode away."

Grace was talking to her through the open window of Alex's pickup. She'd started talking the moment they'd pulled up, not waiting for Alex to shut off the engine.

"We didn't see any cows, though. Not this time." Grace hopped out of the truck and gave the door a pat after closing it. "But we brought the truck, just in case. We can drive off the road if we have to go around a cow again."

Sophia nodded some more, so full of emotion at seeing her sister that she wasn't really listening to what she was saying. It was just so good to see her face. She'd missed her so much.

Sophia hesitated at the edge of the flagstone. Her sister had been so adamant that Sophia should only call for an emergency, and Grace hadn't called her once, not one single time in the past week to ask how she was doing.

Was this how their relationship was supposed to be now? Polite and friendly visits once a week?

Sophia wanted to run to her sister and give her a bear hug. Instead, she twisted her fingers together as she kept nodding and smiling.

Alex got out of his side of the truck and spoke to Grace. "Sophia looks like she missed you almost as much as you missed her. Is one of you going to hug the other, or what?"

"You missed me?" Sophia asked, but Grace couldn't answer because she'd already run up to the patio and thrown her arms around her.

"I've been so worried about you," Grace said, hugging her hard.

Sophia took a split second to think before blurting out something snarky. *Yeah, I could tell by the way you totally ignored me.*

She pulled back from the hug just far enough to smooth Grace's dark gold hair into place, a gesture that went back to their tween years, when they'd first started playing with curling irons and hair spray. "When you're worried about me, you could give me a call. I'd love to hear from you."

"But—but I have called you. A lot."

"The phone hasn't rung once. I just assumed you were busy with your new job and with…" She gestured toward Alex, who was standing beside the truck. Then Sophia realized she'd made it sound like Grace was busy getting busy with Alex, which wasn't a great thing to think about her sister, even if it was probably true.

Sophia almost blushed. "I mean, with your wedding planning. I thought you were busy planning your wedding." *Without me.*

"I called, but you never picked up, so I figured you didn't want to talk. Or maybe I was calling you too late at night."

"I'm up all night long. I'm taking care of a kitten. It needs fed every two hours. It's pretty exhausting, but I volunteered for it, so…"

"You did?" Grace's amazement was genuine. She wasn't an actor.

Sophia was. She pretended not to be hurt that her sister was amazed she would volunteer to sacrifice her sleep for something besides herself. For years, Sophia had cared for Grace, but the freshest memory was obviously of Sophia blowing off everyone and everything for wild parties.

"It's just for a few days," Sophia said, a brilliant performance of perfect cheerfulness. She didn't sound offended at all, not hurt one bit. "The vet is scheduled to come out then, and Travis is sure he'll know a mother cat somewhere that just had a litter and can take another kitten. This one is so young, its eyes aren't even open yet, so it really needs a cat mother, not me."

"Wow. I'm so impressed. I had no idea you knew so much about cats." Grace gave her arm an extra squeeze. "But I'm not surprised. You've always been able to do anything you set your mind to."

Sophia didn't know what to say to that. It sounded like her sister still admired her. Considering the front-row seat she'd had to Sophia's self-destructing spiral, that was something of a miracle.

Sophia didn't want to start bawling and ruin a perfectly lovely conversation. She blinked away the threatening tears and focused on the barn. "I got a crash course on cats from Travis. The foreman you waved at."

"He promised me he'd check on you. He has, hasn't he?"

Sophia nodded some more and wished he was here to check on her now. It would be nice for him to see that her sister didn't hate her. He'd only seen them together that first day, snapping at each other over a cow on the road.

Well, Sophia had been doing most of the snapping. Travis must think Sophia was the world's worst sister.

Alex was standing back, giving them some personal space. He really was a pretty decent guy. Handsome, too, in a doctor-like, Clark Kent kind of way.

He turned toward the barn. "Speaking of Travis, is he around? Where is everyone?"

"It's May." Sophia said it the way Travis would.

"What does that mean?"

She shrugged. "I have no earthly idea, but it's the answer to everything around here. Apparently, cowboys are scarce on a ranch in May."

"Or else they're out working on the range," Alex said. "I think its calving season. We get a few injuries in the ER every year at this time from roundups."

"I'm dying to see this kitten." Grace sounded as carefree as Sophia could remember her sounding since the day their parents had died. Alex must be more than just a decent guy, because Sophia knew she hadn't taken any burdens from Grace's shoulders, not lately. Alex must have lightened that load.

He picked up some grocery bags from the bed of the pickup. "Let's get these inside and check the ringer on that phone. I don't want you two to miss any more calls."

Sophia reached for one of the bags, but Alex shook his head. "It's okay. I've got it."

"Thank you." She meant for more than the groceries. Could he tell?

He winked at her, his eyes blue like her own. Like a brother might have had, if she'd ever had a brother. "She's happier when you're part of her life. I want Grace to be happy, you know."

"I know."

"Let's go fix that dinosaur of a phone."

Grace opened her cab door and reached for a basket. "I almost forgot. Our neighbor grows vegetables, and you wouldn't believe how much zucchini he had. I brought you some. You don't see this in LA. Isn't it great?"

"Oh, zucchini. Yes. Great."

If she could point at a mattress and smile for fifty bucks, she could certainly beam at a basket of zucchini that her sister thought would make her happy. Apparently, the gift of love in Texas during the month of May was zucchini, whether it was from a mother to a ranch hand, from Travis to her, from Grace to—

From Travis to her?

It would be crazy to think he loved her, just because he'd left her a batch of zucchini.

With a note that said he didn't want her to get any more scars.

As she held the door open for her family with one hand and balanced an overflowing basket of zucchini with the other, she couldn't help but look at the empty barn one more time.

A gift of love? She was being too dramatic again—but something felt different now. The zucchini had marked some kind of turning point. Before, Travis would have expected her to do something simple yet impossible: *if you need milk replacer, go to the feed store*. Instead, he'd sent Braden to get it.

It was almost June. May had been full of loneliness and failure and zucchini. But June might be different. A new month. A new vegetable? A new chance to spend time with Travis.

She could hardly wait for June.

Chapter Eleven

Tomatoes.

June was only half over, but if Sophia saw another tomato, she might scream. Or barf.

It turned out the potted plants lining one side of the flagstone patio were Mrs. MacDowell's absurdly fertile tomatoes. There were so many, they ripened and fell off the vines, bounced out of their pots and split open on the patio, where they proceeded to cook on the hot stone in the June sun. Every deep yoga breath Sophia took brought in shimmering molecules of hot energy that smelled vaguely like lasagna.

The smell made her stomach turn.

She'd had such high hopes for June. She'd imagined basking in the sun, breathing deeply, feeling the health and strength of every muscle in her body as she went through all the yoga routines she could remember. Travis wouldn't be able to resist spying on her. Drooling over her silver-screen-worthy body, he would spend lots of time with her, and she wouldn't be lonely in the least.

Instead, she was the one who drooled over Travis, spying on him from the kitchen window. June had brought him back from wherever he'd been disappearing to, but although he spent part of every day in the barn, he was never alone. The ranch must be too big for just one person, because there were always other cowboys around. Usually, they left in pairs on horseback, off to do whatever the heck kept ranchers busy in the month of June.

Her eye was always drawn to Travis. She knew the way he sat a horse now, the set of his shoulders, the way a coil of rope always rested on the back of his saddle when he rode away, the way the rope was looped on the saddle horn and resting on top of his right thigh when he returned.

Not today. She heard what sounded like a motorcycle.

She ran to the window in time to catch Travis roaring away on an ATV. He was in jeans and a plaid shirt, as usual, but he wore no hat to keep the wind out of his hair. He drove the four-wheeler the way he galloped a horse, almost standing up, leaning over the handlebars into the wind. He looked so strong and young and free, something in her yearned to be with him.

"Wait for me." But saying the words out loud didn't make them seem any less pitiful than when they echoed in her head.

She put her hand on the glass, well and truly isolated. If only a director would yell *cut*. If only the prop team would help her out of a mock space capsule. If only Grace were waiting to bring her out of her self-induced sorrow, to remind her that it was only a movie, and the real Sophia could have a bowl of ice cream and paint her fingernails and never, ever have to wonder if she'd make it back to Earth.

Normalcy. It had always been such a relief to return to the normal world after experiencing a character's intense emotions. Now her real life was the unrealistic one, and her old, normal life was the fantasy.

As Travis rode away, Sophia kept her greedy eyes on him and indulged her favorite fantasy, the one where she wasn't famous yet and had no reason to hide. If she and Travis had met when she was nineteen instead of twenty-nine, she would have flirted outrageously with him. As a young cowboy, he wouldn't have been able to resist letting her hitch a ride to the barn on the running board of his ATV. She would've been the best part of his day, his pretty blond girlfriend holding on to him so she wouldn't fall off while he drove. He would've saved up his money to take her to the movies.

"Cut," she whispered to herself.

In real life, she was the one in the movies, a Hollywood star who couldn't hide forever. There was no stopping the fame now. She couldn't make people forget her face.

"No, really. Cut, before you drive yourself crazy."

She pushed hard with her hand, forcing herself away from the window. She was dressed for a morning yoga workout, but she hadn't kept track of where the ranch hands were. There were five different guys who showed up at least a few days each week. Who had shown up for work with Travis today? Was anyone still in the barn?

She couldn't go out to the patio if someone else might still be around. A few minutes of inattention while she'd wallowed in self-pity had cost her. Now she was stuck inside for the day. She'd already watched all of Mrs. Mac-Dowell's DVDs and had browsed through some of her bookshelves. There were a lot of Hardy Boy volumes. The cover of a pregnancy handbook was so laughably 80s, Sophia had quickly shoved it back onto the shelf. There were a lot of cookbooks. She could give the air conditioner a workout by heating up the kitchen as she tried every single tomato recipe.

The sound of the ATV's engine surprised her. She glued her nose right back to the window. Travis was driving back at a more sedate pace, hauling a trailer full of square hay bales behind the four-wheeler, but there was nothing sedate about his appearance, nor its effect on her. His shirt was unbuttoned all the way, flaring out behind him like a plaid cape.

Sophia bet it was no big deal for him. The day was hot, the drive was easy, why not unbutton his shirt and let the air cool his chest? But for her, it was a very big deal. The sexual turn-on was instant, a primitive response to the visual stimulation of a man's strong body. Six-pack abs in low-slung jeans were a big *yes* in her mind. Weeks ago, when Travis had come into the barn dripping wet, she'd felt that same instant, heavy wanting.

It was heavier now, because now she knew Travis, the man with the hands that handled kittens and controlled horses. The man with the voice that never tried to shout her down. The man who'd listened when she poured her heart out, then gifted her with those three little words she hadn't known she'd needed to hear: *I get it.*

And yeah, the man with six-pack abs. Hot damn, he looked good. Really good.

He was looking right at her.

She jerked away and dropped the curtain, as if he'd pointed a telephoto zoom lens at her.

That was a mistake. Now he was going to think she was embarrassed, as if he'd caught her spying on him.

He had.

Okay, so she'd been spying on him, but she should have played it cool, like she'd just happened to be looking out the window, checking the weather. It was probably too little, too late, but she did that now, using the back of her hand to lift the curtain oh-so-casually. *Hot and sunny, not a cloud in the sky. Same as always.*

Travis turned the ATV and started driving it straight toward the house.

Ohmigod, ohmigod, ohmigod. He was coming to say hello. She tried to fix her hair with her fingers. She wasn't wearing makeup, which wasn't ideal, but on the plus side, she was in her yoga clothes. He wouldn't look at her face if she exposed enough skin. She started to take off the loose green cover-up she'd thrown on over her black bra top. But wait—he'd already seen her in the window in the green. She couldn't open the door in a black sports bra now. Too obvious.

The engine went silent. Sophia peeked out the window and saw six feet of rugged male beauty striding toward her, buttoning his shirt as he came. He started high on his chest, bringing the shirt together with a single button. Then the next one lower. One button after the other, he narrowed the amount of exposed flesh until only one triangle of tanned skin flashed above his belt buckle, and then that was gone, too.

She steadied herself with a hand on the doorknob. If he took those clothes off with as much swagger as he put them on...

The knock on the door was firm. Suddenly, so was her resolve. She wasn't a giddy nineteen-year-old. She was twenty-nine, and she guessed Travis was around thirty. They were consenting adults, and after the sight she'd just witnessed, she couldn't think of a single reason why she shouldn't smile when she opened the door.

Her isolation had taken a turn for the better.

Travis was here. There was nowhere else she'd rather be.

* * *

"Howdy, stranger. Long time, no see."

Sophia Jackson purred the words as she opened the door.

Travis raised an eyebrow.

She draped herself against the door jamb as if she had all the time in the world. Her thin green top draped itself over her curves. She watched the effect that had on him with a knowing look in her eyes.

Yeah, she knew how good she looked. Travis put his hand on the door jamb above her head. He had no idea why the sex goddess was back, but it sure made ten in the morning on a Tuesday a lot more interesting.

"It's about time you came." She said it so suggestively, Travis knew she was teasing. Her eyes were crinkling in the corners with the smile she was holding back. "You told Grace and Alex you'd check on me. Are you here to hold up your part of the bargain?"

Her gaze roamed over him from head to toe, lingering somewhere around the vicinity of his belt before returning to his face. She'd done so before, after he'd hosed off at the barn. That time, she'd been serious and a little bit scared. This time, she was having fun, evaluating him as nothing more than a hunk of meat. Treating him as nothing more than eye candy.

He liked it.

But he didn't trust it. He waited for that moment of hesitation, her fear of this attraction they shared.

He didn't see it, so he played along, answering her question as seriously as she'd asked it. "A man's got to work sometimes. It's only been forty-eight hours since I talked to you."

She pouted prettily, picture-perfect. "But Grace and Alex were here for their little weekly visit at the same time. It doesn't count as checking on me when they're already checking on me."

"I'll keep that in mind." He shifted so that he leaned his forearm instead of his hand on the frame of the door. It brought him into her personal space. As they talked about nothing, he watched her the same way he'd watch a yearling when he approached her with bridle in hand for the first time.

Sophia didn't flinch from his nearness. "If you didn't come to check me out, then I have to warn you that this house is no longer accepting zucchini donations."

"I'm glad to hear it, because there aren't any left. Someone snuck into the barn and conspired with my horses to dispose of the rest."

She laughed and stood up straight, done with the exaggerated come-hither routine. She was still a sex goddess, whether she tried to be or not.

He stayed lounging against her door frame. "Samson incriminated you. I found zucchini in his stall. I'm surprised he ate any of it. Most horses aren't particularly fond of it, or else people around here would probably grow even more of it than they do now."

"I guess it all depends who's doing the feeding. Maybe some hands have just the right touch."

He didn't know why she was so lighthearted today, but she was irresistible in this mood.

It was a dangerous word, *irresistible*. He could imagine a future with an irresistible woman, but not with a celebrity. Sophia wouldn't be staying in his life, which was one reason he'd been staying away. He needed to enjoy this conversation for what it was and not think about what it might have led to in different circumstances.

"I'll see if Samson likes tomatoes tonight," she said.

"They're going rotten because I can't cook them fast enough."

He got a little serious. "Don't do that. Tomato plants aren't good for horses."

She got a little serious, too. "Okay, I won't. I guess I would've figured it out when they spit them back out at me."

"They might have eaten them. Horses don't always have the sense to stay away from something that might hurt them."

And neither, he realized, did he.

"I didn't know," she said.

"Now you do."

"Déjà vu. Now I know fridges have casters and horses can't eat tomatoes."

He didn't have anything to say to that. If they were a couple, he would've dropped a sweet kiss on her lips and gone back to work. He would've anticipated having her alone tonight, a leisurely feast. Or hard and intense. Or emotional and gentle—any way they wanted it.

She bit the lip he was lusting after, but she looked concerned, not carnal. "So, if you didn't come under orders to check on me, why are you here? I hope the two kittens are okay. I looked when I went to the barn last night, but I couldn't find them at all."

Kittens. Right. He forced his thoughts to change gear.

"The mother moves them every day. She's a skittish one, but the two kittens are doing fine."

Sophia wrinkled her nose, instantly repulsed. "She's a terrible mother. I lost a lot of sleep because of her. I'm glad your vet found a new mother for the one she abandoned."

It was interesting, the way she hadn't forgiven that poor cat for isolating one of her kittens. "In my business, any time offspring are thriving without my help, then the mother's all right. Some cats make one nest and stick to it for a month, some move their kittens around twice a day. The bottom line is that there are two kittens in that barn I don't have to worry about, so she's good enough in my book. Don't be so hard on her."

Sophia put a bright smile on her face, a fake one, putting her guard up. "So, are there any other cheerful topics you'd like to discuss?"

A cat seemed a strange reason to put up walls. Travis stopped lounging against her door. He'd gotten entirely too comfortable when he had work to do. "I wanted to let you know we're burning off some cedar today. If you look off your front porch and see smoke, you don't have to come check it out."

Now she was the one to raise an eyebrow. "You thought I'd come see what's on fire?"

"You should. It's what you do on a ranch. You look out for each other, remember? You go see why someone's laying on their car horn. If something's burning, you'd better know what it is."

"I'm hiding. I couldn't check it out even if I wanted to, *remember*?"

The hiding was of her own choosing, as far as he could tell. She could decide not give a damn about the paparazzi knowing where she was, and she could decide not to care if they did take her picture. Travis had asked Alex and Grace about the ex during their last visit, and they'd assured him that the DJ was too busy partying in LA to give Sophia a second thought.

Yet Travis had seen Sophia's scars, so he didn't feel free to criticize her. Maybe he'd choose to become a hermit, too, if he walked a mile in her shoes.

He simply nodded to let her know he remembered that she had her reasons. "Now you know that if you see smoke today, it's intentional, for what it's worth. I've got to get back to work."

"Hey, Travis?" she called after him. "Are all your cowboys going to be at the fire? If it's safe for me to go outside, I'd like to go see the horses."

"Even if they can't help you get rid of your tomatoes?"

"I need someone to talk to."

He wished it was a joke.

"Yes, you're safe."

Chapter Twelve

The horses were beautiful.

Sophia had only talked to them when they'd been standing patiently in their stalls at the end of the day. Of course, she'd seen them under saddle, working, but she hadn't seen them like this before.

She only came to the barn after sundown. She hadn't realized the horses spent their day in the pasture or the paddock or whatever this huge, fenced-in field was called. It ran from the barn at one end all the way to the stables at the other, a stretch of maybe a quarter mile. The horses were spread out the entire distance, swishing their tails and nibbling at grass. They looked happy and content, so much so that they paid her no attention as she stood on a fence rail in her sneakers and yoga clothes.

That was okay; she had Grace to talk to.

"This is so pretty. I'm glad I came out here on my day off." Sophia was glad, too. The visit was a total surprise,

which made it all the more special. Alex wasn't here, and
Grace wasn't dutifully delivering groceries. This was just
about them, two sisters who'd rarely been apart before
this year.

Sophia jumped down from the fence and bent to scratch
a black and gray dog behind the ears. When roundup had
ended and all the horses and cowboys had come in, this
dog had come, too, apparently part of the whole gang.
Her name was Patch. Travis called her a cow dog, but she
seemed keen to be with the horses.

"I brought you some of my neighbor's tomatoes," Grace
said. "Don't let me forget to take them out of the trunk before I go. I probably shouldn't have left them in there. The
whole car will smell like tomatoes in this heat."

The mere thought of the smell of tomatoes made Sophia want to gag.

Grace seemed extra talkative today, raving about her
new job at the hospital where Alex worked. She was writing grant proposals and doing something with research
studies, using all the organization skills she'd perfected
as a personal assistant to a celebrity.

Sophia smiled and listened, but inside, she was hurting. Grace apparently had forgotten that her old job had
been to work for Sophia. When she raved about how cool
and great her new boss was, did she not realize that implied her old boss had been not so cool and not so great?

Sophia watched the horses and listened to how much
better Grace's life was without her. She'd almost rather
talk to the horses. She'd never done them wrong. They
didn't care if she was famous or a loser or a famous loser.

"Do you know what I need?" Sophia asked.

Grace went quiet in the middle of her sentence. "What
do you mean?"

"I need boots. Western ones, so I can learn how to ride.

Get me four or five pair and bring them out next Sunday. I'll pick one. I need jeans, too. I've got those shredded Miami ones, but I need regular jeans, like Mom used to buy us. Something less than a thousand dollars. I'm not making any money right now."

"Sophie."

That was all Grace had to say. The warning note said the rest.

Sophia shut up, but Grace gave her the lecture, anyway. "I'm your sister, not your personal assistant. I'm not writing this down in a little notebook anymore, so you can stop dictating to me."

Grace seemed to know what kinds of thing sisters should do compared to what kinds of things personal assistants should do. Sophia didn't see this clear-cut distinction. Grace brought her groceries, for example, but when Sophia had handed her a pile of dirty laundry that first week, Grace had grown quite cool and informed Sophia that the house had a washer and dryer.

"I need a personal assistant. You promised to find me a replacement when you left me for Alex." Sophia didn't care that she sounded petulant. Sisters got petulant.

"I didn't leave you for Alex. I fell in love with Alex, and I still love you, too. I always will. Millions of people love their spouses and their siblings, both. I'm one of them."

She sounded so calm, so infuriatingly right. It reminded Sophia of the way Travis had talked to her, until she'd showed him her scars. "How do you suggest I do my own shopping for boots? You know I can't walk into a store. I could shop online, if I had any internet access. You're going to have to get me a laptop or a smartphone. Then I could be independent."

Grace bit her lower lip, a habit that Sophia knew she still did as well. She knew, because cameras caught everything.

"I don't think having internet access would be a good idea," Grace said.

"Why not?"

Grace couldn't quite look her in the eye. "Hackers will use it to find you."

"That's not the whole story, is it? What's on the internet that you don't want me to see?"

"It's just…things haven't really died down the way we'd hoped. Not yet. But they will. Um…when do you want to tell Deezee you're pregnant? Alex and I want to be—"

"I'm not pregnant." There. Those words felt much better out loud than rattling around in her head.

"What?" Grace's arm was suddenly around her shoulder. Her voice was all sympathy, shopping and laundry and every other offense forgotten. "Oh, Sophie. When did you miscarry? Why didn't you tell me?"

"I didn't. I was never pregnant in the first place. The tests can be wrong, you know. It says so in the instructions."

"So you got your period this month?"

That startled Sophia. She hadn't been paying attention, really, but she quickly counted the weeks up in her head. They couldn't be right.

She shrugged. "I don't feel pregnant. Look at me. Does this look like a pregnant woman's body?"

Grace looked at her, but not at her stomach. She smoothed Sophia's hair over her shoulder with an almost painful gentleness. The expression on Grace's face was unbearable. Concern, compassion, pity—just horrible.

Sophia turned back to the pasture and shaded her eyes with her hand. "Where's Samson? Do you see him? He's the big bay with black points." She forced a laugh. "Aren't you impressed with my cowgirl talk? That's just a horsey way to say brown with black trim. Travis left the ATV here. I bet he took Samson out for the day. Anyhow, Samson just loves Jean Paul's shampoo. When I get back to LA, I'm going to ship a gallon of it to the ranch."

"Sophia—"

"Just so he has it to remember me by."

"Sophia, you're pregnant."

She whirled to face her sister. "I am not. I wish I'd never done that test in the first place. It's just making everyone worry over nothing."

"You've missed two periods and had a positive pregnancy test."

Sophia kept her chin high. The fence rail was solid under her hands. She wasn't going to crack. She wasn't going to fall apart.

"I'm not, but it wouldn't matter if I was."

"It matters to me," Grace said.

"I had to get out of the spotlight for a little while, anyway, right? If I am pregnant, which I'm not, then I already told you the plan. I'll just have the baby and give it up for adoption."

"Why would you do that?"

"Why wouldn't I? Some couple is out there just dying to have a baby. I'd be a surrogate mother. That's a really noble thing to do, you know."

"But you're not a surrogate mother. This is actually your baby."

"I don't want to talk about it." She started walking toward the barn, done with the whole conversation, angry at her sister for bringing it up.

Patch stayed with the horses, but Grace dogged her heels. "Well, I do want to talk about it. It's the whole reason I came out here today."

Sophia nearly tripped on those words. She'd been suckered into thinking that Grace had sought her out because she wanted to be her sister and her friend, but it was just a betrayal. She didn't want Sophia's company. It had all been a trap to force Sophia to talk about something she didn't even want to think about.

Sophia broke into a run, sneakers pounding relentlessly into the ground until she reached the barn. Until she reached the office. Until she threw herself into Travis's chair.

"Sophie! Where are you?" Grace stopped in the office doorway, breathless. "Don't do this."

"Do what? Not talk about something I don't want to talk about? If I'm pregnant, it has no bearing on you."

"Yes, it does. I'm trying to plan a wedding. My wedding. And I came here today because I wanted to ask you to be my maid of honor."

Sophia closed her eyes. She'd hated herself plenty of times before, but this one was the worst.

"But we need to talk about your pregnancy." Grace had tears in her voice. "I tried to be flexible. I chose a bunch of different locations, but the soonest I could book any of them was September. You'll be showing in September."

"And you don't want a pregnant cow in your wedding." Sophia murmured the words more to herself than to Grace.

"No. That isn't it at all. If you were keeping your baby, then it wouldn't matter at all that you were showing. You'd have nothing to hide."

Grace took a deep breath, and Sophia knew she was about to hear something she didn't want to hear.

"But if you want to keep everything a secret, then I have to respect that. I tried guesstimating when you were due and how long it would take for your body to recover so that people wouldn't suspect you'd ever had a baby. If you're due in January, I think you probably wouldn't be comfortable trying to pull it off until April, even with the way you work out. I don't want to wait until next April to marry Alex. I want my big sister in my wedding, but it's not just about having a white gown and a party and some photos. It's about actually being married to Alex. I want to make him those promises now. I want to start our lives together now, not next year."

Sophia knew she was supposed to say something, but she had nothing to contribute. Grace had thought everything through while Sophia had refused to think of it at all.

"If you don't want to be seen, I thought about asking someone else to stand up with me. I've made some friends, and...well, I really like Kendry MacDowell. She's married to Alex's department chair, Jamie MacDowell. When Alex was putting out feelers about finding a place off the beaten path, Jamie mentioned his mother's house was vacant, so that's how we found this place for you. His baby picture is on the wall in your house, isn't that funny? Anyway, his wife Kendry is my age, and—"

"I understand." Sophia didn't want to hear it. Neither she nor Grace had been able to make friends outside their two-sister world, not when deli clerks were bribed to expose them. She knew she should be happy for Grace, but she didn't want to hear how Kendry was going to hold Grace's bouquet while Alex put a gold band on Grace's finger and started a new life with her.

Her little Grace had lost the best mother. She'd gotten a skittish big sister as a poor substitute. But Grace wasn't letting anything get in her way now. She was doing so much better out of the nest on her own than she ever had when Sophia had dragged her around the world in pursuit of Hollywood dreams.

"I'm so sorry," Sophia said. She was. About everything.

"Don't be sorry. The wedding will be great. We're thinking about a ceremony earlier in the day. We found the cutest bridesmaid dresses, this lemon yellow that's short and swingy. It would be great for a daytime wedding. Kendry's expecting, too. She's further along than you are, so we were excited to find a dress that will work. Even though it's not a maternity dress, it will look cute on her."

Stop. Please, stop.

Sophia couldn't act her way out of this. *Kendry's expecting,* her sister said, like it was a good thing, something to look forward to. If it turned out that Sophia was really pregnant, there would be no excitement, only plans for damage control.

"It would look really cute on you, too. It's only June. You might change your mind by September. You could be in the wedding, too."

Sophia could only shake her head, a vehement denial, as her tears began falling.

She looked around the office, but there wasn't a tissue box in this male space. She already knew there were textbooks on crops and cows, a computer she couldn't access. There was a baseball on the shelf above the neat stack of T-shirts.

Sophia grabbed Travis's T-shirt and mopped up her face.

"Oh, don't cry, Sophie." Grace's voice was husky with her own tears, a sound Sophia remembered from those awful nights when they'd grieved together. "I just wanted... I wanted to talk to you in person. I've tried to ask you about it before, but you wouldn't...well, at some point, I just had to make the call, so we put the deposit down on this rooftop venue for September."

Sophia stood up, clutching Travis's shirt close in case she couldn't pull off the greatest acting job in her life. "September sounds like a good time of year for something outdoors on a rooftop. It won't be as hot as it is now."

Grace looked so concerned. Sophia was being as unselfish as she could. The least Grace could do was let herself be fooled by the act.

"This is just one day out of our whole lives," Grace said. "It doesn't change anything between us. We're sisters."

"Always." But Sophia felt a little frantic. She wanted to get out of the barn and go somewhere else. Be someone else.

Travis had a digital clock on the wall, the kind that gave barometric pressure and humidity and a lot of other stuff that wouldn't matter to Sophia once she gave up and went back to bed. "Look at the time. I have to go back to the house before anyone comes in from the range. Travis is the only one who knows I'm here. There are other guys working today, and one of them might come in any second."

It was a lie. Travis had told her she'd be safe, but she didn't feel safe. She needed to hide and lick her wounds.

Grace followed her out of the barn. "I've got a little bit of time before I have to go. I'm meeting Kendry at this florist that did her brother-in-law's wedding. Braden's. Do you remember Lana and Braden? They were at your table at the Texas Rescue ball...oh, never mind. Sorry."

"I met them. For about five seconds."

Before Deezee showed up and I made the dumbest decision of my life.

Grace did her best to keep talking as if that hadn't been an awkward reminder of a terrible event.

Sophia let Grace's voice wash over her as they walked side by side in the sunshine. The calm weather made a mockery of Sophia's inner turmoil. If she could just turn back time to the person she'd been before she met Deezee...

She'd thought the same thing after she'd tried to touch Travis's wet body and he'd turned her down cold. She'd been certain the pre-Deezee version of herself would've been more desirable. Yet this morning she'd flirted with Travis, and he'd dropped everything he was doing to stand a little too close to her under that kitchen door awning. He seemed to like the current version after all.

Grace had changed topics from her life to Sophia's. "I don't know how to keep you hidden at ob-gyn appointments, but there are midwives associated with the hospital who make house calls. That might work. They have patient confidentiality rules in place, but I'll look into a more comprehensive confidentiality contract, the kind we had for the housekeepers and staff back in LA."

Before meeting Deezee, Sophia had entrusted her day-to-day routine to her personal assistant, but she'd made all the big decisions herself. She'd set her long-term goals and planned out every strategic move to get there. Her reputation as a smart and savvy actor had been earned. Now, Grace was deciding Sophia's medical care for her.

"I'm worried about the press, though," Grace said. "If they wanted to know what you ate so badly, I can't imagine what lengths they'll go to for baby gossip."

Before Deezee, it had never been her assistant's job to decide what to do next. Sophia had never put that burden on her sister's shoulders.

"Hey, Gracie?"

They stopped by her sister's car.

"You've got enough on your plate without worrying about doctors and confidentiality and all the rest. I'm going to look into it."

"Are you sure? I was going to try making some anonymous calls to a few adoption agencies to see what's involved—"

"Stop, sweetie." Sophia took a deep breath. "You've been an absolute rock for me, but I've got this, okay? I can make the calls, if and when I need to. You, meanwhile, are the bride, and you've got an appointment in town with a florist and some friends. Go."

"Are you sure?"

Sophia nodded. This didn't feel like acting. This felt like being herself. Not her old self, not her new self, just herself.

She used the T-shirt to gesture toward Grace's car as she smiled at her beautiful baby sister. "Go be the bride. Order your flowers. No one will look at them when they can look at a bride like you, but get the prettiest ones you can, anyway."

"Oh, Sophie." But Grace's voice wasn't sad. She was excited. "Thanks for being so understanding. I can't tell you how nervous I was about this. You're the best."

The T-shirt in Sophia's fist couldn't crack. She wouldn't crack, either.

"Oh, I almost forgot." Grace popped her trunk with a press of the button on her key fob. "Look, a whole basket of tomatoes for you."

Chapter Thirteen

We got a visitor.

The text message hit his phone when Travis walked away
from the burning pile of cedar saplings. Cell phones were
unreliable like that out here. One part of an empty field
could get a cell signal and another part couldn't.

The text was from Clay, who was working at the pond
near the edge of the property that bordered the road to
Austin. The time stamp indicated the text was two hours
old, just now reaching his phone.

His cell phone pinged again, receiving another text.

Same car as Sunday.

Grace or Alex had come to see Sophia, then.

Travis put the cell phone back in his pocket. He felt like
more of a forester than a rancher today, since he'd been

swinging an ax instead of throwing a lasso. It had to be done, though. The cedar could destroy a pasture in a matter of years, multiplying and spreading roots that would hog all the water and kill the grass his cattle needed for forage.

Another ping sounded, rapidly followed by more, all the texts that had been lined up, waiting for a satellite to find his phone.

Got another visitor.

The time was ten minutes ago. The text had been sent to all the men working the River Mack today.

Blue 4-door sedan? Anyone know it?

No.

No.

When Travis's voice mail played its alert sound, he was already halfway to the shade tree where he'd left Samson.

He listened to Clay's message as he walked. "We got a visitor, boss. I'm too far away to get a good look, but I don't know the car. It doesn't look like it belongs here. I'm knee-deep at the pond. Might be faster if you could meet 'em at the next gate."

There were three sets of gates on the road that led to the house. The main gate was the one Clay had seen. The second set of gates were about a mile and a half farther into the ranch itself, and the third set of gates were a mile closer to the house from there.

This year's new ranch hand, always called the green-horn, was standing with a shovel near the fire, his phone in his hand. Clearly, he'd just gotten the texts, too, and was reading.

"You want me to come with you?" he called to Travis, with all the excitement of a first-year cowboy in his voice.

"You can't leave a fire unattended," Travis reminded him as he untied Samson's reins.

"I'm gonna miss all the fun."

"Greenhorns aren't supposed to have fun."

He swung himself into the saddle. His horse's idea of fun was to be given his head so he could run, so Travis pointed Samson toward the ranch road and let him go with a sharply spoken *gid-yap*. They covered the mile or so to the second set of gates in a handful of minutes. The blue car had gone through the gate, but it was still there, waiting for its passenger to close the gate and get back in.

Travis reined in Samson, then walked him to the middle of the road and stopped a little distance away from the car. He didn't recognize it. More than that, he didn't like the look of the man that was closing the gate—or rather, he didn't like the camera that the man held in one hand. It had a two-foot-long lens that looked like it was compensating for some shortcomings in some other department. That, or the man was a professional photographer.

"What's your business here, gentlemen?"

The cameraman looked absolutely dumbfounded to see a cowboy on a horse in the middle of the road. City folk. What did they expect to see on a ranch?

The driver stuck his head out the window. "You're in the way. Move."

Travis didn't bother answering that.

The driver threw up a hand. "What do you want?"

"I just asked you that."

"We're going to see a friend of ours."

That lie didn't really deserve an answer, but Travis supposed he needed to spell things out for them. "You can turn your car around and head back the way you came."

"We're not leaving," the cameraman said. "We're not doing anything wrong."

"That's not for you to decide. You're on private property."

"What's your name?" the cameraman demanded, as if he had the right to know.

That definitely didn't deserve an answer.

The cameraman lifted the huge lens and took a few photos of Travis. "We'll identify you."

It would be humorous if they showed the photos to the local sheriff to file a complaint against him. Travis knew the sheriff and most of the deputies, of course, but it was more than that. This was Texas cattle country. The rules had been in place here for well more than a century. If a cattleman didn't want you on his property, then you got off his property. The sheriff would laugh these men out of his office for complaining about a foreman doing his job.

The driver pulled his head back into his car. Stuck it out the window again. "C'mon, Peter. Get in the car."

Once the cameraman was in, the driver revved the engine. He inched the vehicle forward, then revved the engine some more.

Pushy little bastards.

So these were paparazzi. Had to be. Travis imagined it would be a nuisance to have them following him and taking pictures while he walked down a public street. Coming onto someone else's land and sticking a camera in their face took nuisance to a different level. Trespassing was illegal. Trespassing and then taking photographs took a lot of gall.

Years of this would wear on a person. Travis had a better idea now of just how much it had worn on Sophia.

The car lurched forward a full car length, rushing his horse before slamming on its brakes. Samson threw his head up and gave it the side-eye, but he stayed under control. Travis gave him a solid pat on the neck, turned in his saddle, and pulled his hunting rifle out of its carrying case. He pulled a single bullet out of the cardboard box he kept in his saddlebag.

Carrying a rifle was part of Travis's job. Predators had to be dealt with; they'd found the remains of a calf that had been lost to a predator just yesterday. Travis would never kill a man over photographs, but he'd never let a car kill a horse, either. If he were to fire this weapon, every cowboy in hearing distance would come to check it out. If Travis happened to fire that signal shot in the direction of one of the car's tires, well, things like that happened.

One thing that wasn't going to happen? These men weren't getting any closer to Sophia.

Travis opened the rifle's chamber. Empty, as it should be unless he was about to use it. He slipped the bullet into place and locked the bolt into position. It made a satisfying metallic sound for the benefit of the trespassers. Travis set the rifle across his thighs and waited.

The driver and the cameramen started making incredulous hand gestures. Then the driver laid on the horn, nice and loud. Nice and long.

Travis smiled. Wouldn't be long now.

Clay had already been on his way, so he arrived first. A few minutes later, Buck, a young hand working his second year on the River Mack, rode up. Buck was as good-natured and laid-back as they came, but between the text messages and the car horn, he arrived looking serious. The men stayed on their horses, flanking Travis.

"This road's getting mighty crowded," Travis said.

The driver laid on the horn again, longer and louder.

"Seems rude," Clay said.

"Doesn't he?"

The driver got out of the car. "This is very interesting. What are you guys hiding? Why don't you want us to visit our friend?"

"We may be here awhile," Travis said to his men. "He doesn't understand the concept of private property."

The driver addressed Travis's men, too. "Either of you fellas know Sophia Jackson?"

Well, hell. Now it was like playing poker. Travis had to act like he didn't know the cards he held in his own hand.

"Her sister lives here in Austin. We spotted the sister coming out of a bridal shop, then she drove out here to this ranch." The driver squinted at Clay. "Isn't that interesting?"

"Not particularly."

Travis would have to call Alex this evening and let him know Grace was being followed.

"Rumor has it that Sophia Jackson's sister is planning a wedding on this ranch." He made a show of taking his wallet out of his back pocket. "We're just looking for a little confirmation."

"The movie star?" Buck was genuinely incredulous. "What in the hell is this man talkin' about?"

"I believe he thinks we run a catering service," Travis deadpanned. "You cater any weddings lately?"

Buck laughed, although Travis doubted he'd been that funny. Buck just liked to laugh.

The cameraman gestured to his grandiose lens. "Look, I'm just trying to do my job. To capture all the beauty of a wedding, I need to scope out the venue first. Is there a gazebo? Will there be a reception tent? Is Sophia Jackson going to be the maid of honor?"

Buck leaned around Travis to speak to Clay. "I thought you were digging an irrigation ditch today. Didn't know you built weddin' gazebos for movie stars." He cracked himself up with his own joke.

The driver, however, got impatient or insulted. It didn't matter which. What mattered was that he shoved his wallet back in his pants and got behind the wheel again. With his hand on the horn, he put his car in gear. It rolled toward the horses slowly but relentlessly.

Buck stopped laughing.

"Is he playing chicken with us?" Clay asked no one in particular.

Travis didn't believe in playing chicken. He didn't like trespassers, and he didn't like horses being threatened with a car that could kill them. He picked up the rifle, sighted down the barrel, and fired.

The front left tire deflated instantly.

"Never did like games," Travis said, using thigh and knee to keep Samson calm after the gunfire.

"It's about to get real," Clay murmured.

"Yep."

The driver started shouting, jumping out of his car and waving his arms like a caricature of a New York taxi driver. The cameraman got out and started photographing his flat tire.

"Make sure you get my gate in the background, so you can explain to the sheriff how far onto private property you were when your tire blew up." Travis turned to flip his saddlebag open and get another bullet out of the cardboard box. "I'll say this one more time: turn your car around and get off my ranch."

"But you shot out my tire. You *shot* it." The driver was more incredulous about that than Buck had been about movie stars.

"You got a spare, don't you?" Travis pulled back the bolt

on the rifle and chambered another round. "How many spares you got?"

Clay nodded toward the west. "Company's coming."

Travis glanced at the two riders coming toward them with their horses at an easy trot. "Good. Haven't seen Waterson in a while." He looked back at the driver. "You get to changing that tire. We have some visiting to do."

It took the driver and cameraman longer to figure out how to get their spare out of the trunk and set up the jack than it did for Luke Waterson and one of his hands to reach the road. Luke was one of the owner-operators of the James Hill ranch, which bordered the River Mack.

He rode up to Travis and shook hands. "Happened to be in the neighborhood when I heard someone's car horn get stuck. Then the gunshot made it interesting."

"Nice of you to stop by."

"What do we have here?"

Travis leaned his forearm on the pommel of his saddle, keeping the rifle in his other hand pointed away from men and horses. "I believe this here is what you'd call the paparazzi."

"Paparazzi? Which one of you is famous?"

As the men laughed, Travis spoke under his breath to Luke. "Mrs. MacDowell has a houseguest."

"I see." Luke *tched* to his horse and turned him in a circle, until he stood beside Travis. "Looks like we'll be staying until these paparazzi can get their tire changed and get on their way. How long do you think that'll take?"

"They're a little slow on the uptake," Travis said. "I'm gonna say twenty minutes."

"I'll take fifteen."

Clay was skeptical. "Ten bucks says thirty."

In the end, it took them the full thirty minutes, so Clay collected enough beer money to last him a month. Buck was sent to follow the car out to the county road. Waterson and his man headed back to the James Hill. Clay went back to clearing out pond weeds.

Travis turned his horse toward the house.

He had that impatient feeling again, that need to lay eyes on Sophia. *Need* was perhaps the wrong term. The photographers hadn't made it very far onto the ranch, so there was no need to think she was in any kind of distress. She was probably talking to the horses or taking a nap or even holding those yoga poses that had turned him into a voyeur. Travis *wanted* to see Sophia again.

Want and need were all twisted up inside him when it came to Sophia. If he just checked on her, then he'd be able to put his mind at ease and go back to his routine.

Travis told himself that lie for a mile, until the white pillars of Mrs. MacDowell's front porch came into view, and he saw Sophia standing there, hurling tomatoes at the sky.

Chapter Fourteen

He might as well have been invisible.

He'd turned Samson out to the pasture and put on a fresh shirt. His hair still probably smelled like smoke, but Sophia noticed none of it when Travis walked up the front porch steps and joined her by the white pillars. She didn't acknowledge him at all.

It didn't matter. He leaned against a pillar and felt the tension inside him ease, anyway. She was here. He was here. It felt good.

She continued her little ritual as if she were in the middle of a meditation. She chose a tomato from a basket, examined it carefully, and then threw it with considerable skill.

"Had a bad day?" he asked.

"You could say that."

"I'm about to make it worse."

She paused, tomato cupped in her hand.

"I just met my first paparazzi."

"Oh." Her knuckles turned white on the tomato, but as he watched her, she loosened her grip. "I could crush this, but then I'd have to clean up the stupid mess myself."

"You could throw it."

She did.

"Nice arm," he said.

"My daddy taught me."

Right there, just like that, Travis felt something change. The hard squeeze on his heart was painful.

Standing on the porch less than an arm's length from Sophia, he saw her as a child, one who loved her daddy, a young girl determined to learn how to throw a baseball. She might have had pigtails, or she might have been a tomboy in a ball cap, but she'd been somebody's little girl.

Now she was a too-beautiful woman but a very real person, doing the best she could in the world, same as everyone else. She was mostly kind; she had her flaws.

She was irresistible. And the reason she was irresistible was because he was falling in love with her.

Strangers with cameras came to photograph her because that was a crazy side effect of her job. It had nothing to do with Travis and Sophia, two people standing on a porch, throwing tomatoes.His arm was already warmed up from a day spent chopping trees and handling horses and sighting down a hunting rifle for one easy tire shot. He picked up a tomato and threw it for distance, center-field to home plate.

"Wow," she said.

"My dad taught me."

"Do you see your dad very often?"

Rather than answer, he picked up another tomato. Although he'd played shortstop, he took his time like a pitcher on the mound. Wound up. Threw.

"Now you're just showing off."

He winked at her, as if he were still a young college jock. "I can throw a baseball farther than a tomato."

She picked up another one. Studied it. Threw.

"Why are you killing tomatoes?" he asked.

"I'm sick of them." Her little hiss of anger ended in an embarrassed duck of her chin. "It's wasteful, though, isn't it? But I'm not a bad person. They were just rotting in place, anyway."

His heart hurt for her again, for the way she didn't want to be thought of as a bad person. The little girl had grown up to be defensive for a reason. She was judged all the time, not just for whom she dated, but for how her face looked, what she wore, what kind of sandwich she ate.

"I'll tell you a rancher's point of view. The tomatoes came from the land, and you're putting them back into the land. That's not wasteful. Birds are going to come out of nowhere tonight and have a feast, and I bet you'll see a few tomato plants popping up here next spring. In the catalog of possible sins a person could commit, I'd say throwing a tomato is pretty damn minor. You're not a bad person."

"I won't be here next spring." She sounded wistful. It was a gentle warning as well, whether for herself or for him, to not get too attached.

"I know." He threw another tomato, a sidearm hard to first base to beat the runner.

"So, do you see your dad or not?" she asked.

"Dad and I are on speaking terms again."

"What happened?"

"He slept with a married woman. It wasn't with my mother."

"I'm so sorry." Her voice, her posture, all of it softened toward him. For him. "That must have been awful."

"Tore up two families with one affair. But it's been fifteen years. We talk. Take in a game together when I'm in Dallas. Do you see your dad?"

"My dad passed away. The same instant as my mom, actually. Car crash."

He couldn't pick up another tomato.

"It's been ten years. I was nineteen. I became Grace's legal guardian. She was all I had left. She *is* all I have left. Now she's getting m-married."

The tiny stutter said it all.

"In September." She took a breath, and a little of the actress appeared. "Grace came out here today to tell me she'd set the date. She's planning everything without my help, since I'm kind of a liability in public, with the mob scenes and stuff. She's running her own life. She doesn't need me anymore, and I'm so proud of her for that. I really am. And she's happy and excited and everything a bride should be, and I'm so happy about that, too."

Travis waited.

Sophia traced the edge of the tomato basket with her fingertip. "But deep down, I wish she still needed me, and that, for certain, makes me a bad person."

"No, it doesn't."

It was shockingly easy to pull her into his arms. It was shockingly perfect, the way she fit against his chest. She burrowed into him, her cheek on his collarbone. She brought her arms around his back, as if they'd always hugged away the hurt like this, as if they'd always fit together.

"Who is watching?" she asked. Not *Is anyone watching?* Just *who*.

"No one. It's only three o'clock. The men are working."

He set his cheek against her hair, the scent of her shampoo less dominant than the smell of sunshine. She'd spent the day outdoors, then, not in the dark and the air conditioning.

He savored the smell of her skin as he held her, but the embrace was not entirely about comfort. Hunger demanded attention. Travis felt her breasts soft against his chest, felt the heat of her palm on his shoulder blade, and told himself it was enough.

"The paparazzi aren't watching?"

"They won't be back unless they can afford a lot of new tires. They got a flat. It will happen again. Every time."

Tension spiked in her every muscle. "But they'll be back. They'll keep coming back."

He hushed her with a *shh* and another, the same way he soothed a filly being approached by a rider for the first time. "They think Grace might be scouting out the ranch as a place to have her wedding. When she gets married somewhere else in September, they'll stop wondering if her famous sister will show up out here."

"Oh. That's possible. You might be right."

"Don't sound so surprised."

She lifted her cheek. "Don't be so nice to me."

"It's very easy to be nice to you."

She set her hand on the side of his face, and he closed his eyes at the sweet shock of a feminine touch.

It had been a while since he'd been touched by a woman, but it was more than that. It mattered that it was Sophia's fingertips that smoothed their way over his cheek, Sophia's palm that cupped his jaw. Sophia, Sophia—he couldn't get her out of his head, not since the moment he'd first laid eyes on her.

When her thumb traced his lower lip, he opened his eyes just to see her again.

She looked sad. "This has no future."

"What doesn't?" He knew, but he wanted all the cards spread on the table.

"This thing between us. It has nowhere to go."

"I know." He bent his head, and he kissed her. Like the hug, it was as natural as if they'd always kissed. Of course he would press his lips to hers. Of course.

"I don't know where I'll be a year from now. I don't know where I'll be a month from now."

"I know where you are this moment." He placed a kiss carefully on her upper lip, to stop the tears that were threatening to start. "We have this moment."

She kissed him. Her mouth was soft but her kiss was strong. No hesitation. When he thought he'd like to taste her, she opened her mouth and tasted him. In contrast to her words of warning, she kissed him without any doubts.

He had no doubts, either. If this kiss on the porch was all they could ever have, he still wanted it. He needed one moment, just one moment, to stop denying this power between them. Want and need were the same thing: he needed to kiss her more than he wanted to breathe. He wanted to kiss her more than he needed to breathe.

The slide of her tongue was firm and perfect. It satisfied him deep inside, a moment of relief because that hunger had been answered. *Ah, finally, a kiss.* But then the hunger demanded more.

He wanted to know the shape of her, so he let his hands slide and explore. Her body was softer than it looked when she saluted the sun in those God-blessed yoga clothes. Her muscles were relaxed, languid. He shifted their embrace from one of comfort to one of desire. Her hips pressed against his hardness, a moment of bliss—but then he needed more.

Her hands tugged his hair harder than he'd expected. It was just what he wanted, just what he needed—for a moment. Then greed built like a fire, consuming them both. She rose up on her toes to get closer to him, so he cupped her backside and held her tightly in place.

Not tightly enough. She could still move, and she did, sliding up another inch along his hard body, straining for more as they stood on the porch, reaching for something clothing made impossible.

"I'm gonna lose my mind if you do that again." He was warning her, or he was begging her.

"I know. I know." Her words were panted out, raw with need, no purr, no seduction, nothing deliberate.

Still a sex goddess. *More* of a sex goddess.

She couldn't go higher on her toes, but she tried, hands in his hair, flexing her arms, seeking him. If they were only horizontal, she could slide up his body, and it would all work perfectly. They'd fit together, they'd find the release that was desperately needed now, right now, if only they were horizontal—

"Please." She panted the word against his mouth, and he knew exactly what the rest of the desperate plea was. *Please fix this. Please finish this. Please give me what I need.*

He kept one hand buried in her hair, cupping the back of her head, and watched her intently as he opened the door, waiting to see if that was what she really wanted.

It was; she told him what he needed to hear. "Yes."

She knew what she wanted, and she took the first step, bringing him with her, like a dancer leading with an arm around his waist. Two steps brought them inside, and he slammed the door.

Clothes were coming off. His hands slid under the loose green top to the black spandex underneath, the kind of sports bra that never came off easily, damn it, until he felt the hooks in back, thank God. She made short work of his belt with her sure hands while he unfastened her hooks. Her soft breasts spilled free. He filled his hand with one breast, a moment entirely of touch because he could not see her beneath the green top. Not yet.

He kissed her breast through the shirt. In response, she gasped and her hands on his fly shivered to a stop. She was his. She was perfect. This was all he wanted. Then the hunger roared again, and it wasn't enough.

He scooped her top up and over her head. She was so beautifully cooperative, raising her arms so he could draw the shirt completely off, shaking her wrist for him when the bra stuck there.

Together, they tossed away the barriers. She kicked off her sneakers and went to work on the button of his jeans. He dragged his shirt over his head while trying not to lose sight of her bare breasts, as beautiful as the rest of her, with one tiny, dark freckle on the curve of her left breast, just off center of her cleavage, a sexy imperfection he wanted to savor.

She unzipped his fly and slid her hands beneath the waistband to push his jeans to the floor.

Now she hesitated, but the look on her face was one of desire, not fear. After a pause to enjoy the anticipation, she closed the space between them and pressed her nude body against his.

Yes. Yes and absolutely yes, it felt absolutely right when she wrapped her arms around his shoulders and wrapped her legs around his waist. He lifted her higher, holding her thighs in his hands as she cried an inarticulate sound that meant *yes*, this was what she'd begged him for. They needed to get horizontal soon, needed to find a bed or a couch or hell, the floor would work—

But all Sophia did was take a breath, and it was enough

to align their bodies at just the right angle, with just the right amount of pressure, and he was sheathed inside her.

He rocked backward, leaning against whatever piece of furniture was behind him, completely undone at the sensation. Nothing had ever felt so good, nothing in his life. He couldn't move, couldn't breathe. Sophia was hot and wet and all around him. All his.

Hot and wet, so wet...

He wasn't wearing any protection.

Her breath was in his ear. He rained kisses down her neck. "The pill," he managed to say. "Tell me you're on the pill."

"No. Don't you have a condom?"

He shook his head sharply. It wasn't something a man needed to carry to work on the open range, damn it all to hell.

"Just—wait—don't—" He steeled himself—the coming sensation was going to be climax-worthy, but he couldn't, not without protection—then he cupped her bottom and slid her up and off his body. He was sweating from the effort to keep control, a desperate man. "Do you have a condom? In your suitcase? Anywhere?"

"No. I swore off men. Forever." She unwrapped her legs from his waist but stood on her toes before him, arms still around his neck, their bodies still pressed tightly together. "I didn't know there would be you. I never thought there could be you."

She kissed him again, loving his mouth the way their bodies wanted to be loving. He kissed her the way he couldn't have her, although God knew they were both willing.

Still, knowing she wanted him eased something in his chest, and her skin felt glorious against his skin, so when she ended the kiss, Travis found that he could smile, even tease her. "So when you said this wasn't going any-where…"

She gasped-laughed and smacked his chest, but she was quick with the comeback. "You said we had one moment. It sounded kind of romantic at the time, but…" She made a little *shoo* motion with her hand. "There it was. Hope you enjoyed it."

"Oh, hell no. We're having another moment." There were a hundred ways to please a woman, and he was more than willing to try them all with Sophia.

He pushed her just a foot away, so he could finish step-ping out of boots and jeans. She watched, then she touched, one finger trailing down his arm, then one finger trailing up the hard length of him.

He cursed softly, and she laughed, because she knew exactly what he meant by that curse.

She bit her lower lip. "The MacDowells lived here, right? Three guys. Don't you think they might have left something behind in a nightstand from their college days?"

Travis kicked the jeans out of his way and they held hands, jogging naked together through the house to the bedroom hallway. From one room to the next, he took the nightstand on the left side of each bed, she the right, but their search turned up nothing.

"They would've probably been expired, anyway," she said, hands on her hips, wrinkling her nose in disappoint-ment while she talked to him, as if it were perfectly nat-ural to chat with him in the nude. "Aren't you guys the same age?"

"Give or take a few years. I'm thirty-one, so yeah, we're looking for ten-year-old condoms."

They laughed at themselves, but the sound of an ATV brought them both to the window to steal a peek, side by side.

"The greenhorn's back from the cedar burn."

"Now what?" she asked.

"Now I hope he doesn't notice Samson's out in the paddock, so I won't have to explain where I've been later." Travis ran his hand lightly down her back, marveling again at the dip of her lower back and the curve of her thigh. "Much later, because I'm not leaving now. We've got some creative moments in the immediate future."

She kissed his cheek, such an absurdly innocent move. "You still smell like smoke."

"Had I known the best moment of my life was going to happen today, I would have showered before stopping by to throw tomatoes. And I would have brought a damned condom. Spontaneity isn't my strong suit."

She touched him, fingertips smoothing their way from his smoky hair down his chest. "You could take a shower here, and I could try to figure out just what your strong suit is."

"Is that shower big enough for two?"

"Let's find out."

Shampoo and slippery soap led to more laughter. Hands made discoveries, laughter faded into something more intense. Bodies were finally, shatteringly satisfied. As far as spontaneous moments went, although they'd been caught unprepared for basic necessities, Travis could have no complaints.

When he was dressed once more and walking the familiar path to his house, it wasn't the sex that occupied his thoughts; it was the moment that had come afterward. Under the steady, soothing stream of the shower, he'd cradled her against his body for a long, long time. Neither one of them had wanted to move. The water had run down their skin, and the silence between them had been as powerful as everything that had come before.

He was in love with her.

It could go nowhere. It was a fluke they'd found themselves on the same ranch. She was leaving, had been destined to leave since before she'd arrived.

They'd had their moment.

As he walked into his empty house, he already knew it would never be enough.

Chapter Fifteen

"I'm getting married!"

Sophia smiled at her sister's excitement as she pulled groceries out of a brown paper bag. Eggs, flour, real sugar. Sophia had so much time on her hands and such a plethora of Mrs. MacDowell's old cookbooks, she'd decided to try her hand at baking a few things to supplement her frozen dinners. Besides, she could sneak the results of her successful attempts into the barn after dark. Not for the horses, but for Travis, her secret lover for the past two nights.

And tonight. She would definitely find him again tonight after sunset.

With a little thrill inside that she hoped wasn't obvious, she scooped up the five-pound bags of flour and sugar and headed for the pantry, laughing at her excited bride of a sister. "Yes, I know you're getting married. September twenty-fourth. It will be here before you know it."

"No, I'm getting married in five days, and you're going to be my maid of honor."

Sophia stopped in the middle of the kitchen. "What?"

"Somebody had a big party planned at the place we booked for September, and they canceled it. It's Fourth of July weekend, which might not sound so romantic, but I think it will be special. The rooftop patio overlooks Sixth Street. You can see the Capitol all lit up for the night, and the city will have fireworks going off all around us."

"But that's less than a week away. A wedding in a week?" Sophia held the ten pounds of flour and sugar steadily as she stared at Grace. "Is that even possible?"

"The florist said she could do it. The corporation that canceled their party had already booked a bartender and music, so we're just scooping up the people they had reserved. Kendry and Jamie weren't going out of town for the holiday, anyway, so I have my bridesmaid and Alex has his best man. If you're in the wedding, then Alex wants to ask his friend Kent to be a groomsman, so we'll have two girls, two guys. Please say yes. It's perfect."

Alex came in the kitchen door. "I found Travis."

And then Travis was right there, hanging his hat on the hook, and Sophia wasn't sure how to act.

Travis had left her bed at dawn in order to get to the barn before his men, or so he hoped. She wondered if he'd made it there first. If he hadn't, then she wondered how he'd explained arriving from the direction of the MacDowells' house and not from his own. Had anyone arrived early from the bunkhouse?

She couldn't tell from Travis's face whether that had happened or not. He stood near the door with his usual impassive cowboy demeanor, but Sophia knew what he looked like when he laughed. She also knew what he looked like when he was at his most primitive, head thrown back, muscles straining, powerless to stop the climax she'd brought him to.

The flour slipped from her arm. She hitched it back up.

Alex looked like a very pleased Clark Kent. "So Grace told you the big news?"

"Just a second ago. I hardly know what to think."

Alex explained to Travis. "We're getting married this weekend."

"Congratulations." Travis stole a look at Sophia. He knew about September. She'd been throwing tomatoes, wishing her sister needed her in September. She hadn't wanted her sister to need her this badly, though. Not badly enough to ruin her own wedding.

"Are you sure this is what you want?" Sophia asked Grace. "There was nothing wrong with September. I'm afraid you're not going to have the wedding you want if you try to cram this in on short notice. What about your cake? What about your dress?"

"There was something definitely wrong with September. You weren't going to be there. You were so nice about it, but when I drove away, I didn't even make it halfway to Austin before I started crying."

"You seemed so happy when you left."

"Well, a hard conversation was over. You'd been so generous about it all, but I realized that I was settling for something I didn't want. I want you in my wedding. I started feeling kind of sorry for myself, that because of the paparazzi and all the pressure you're always under, I wouldn't get my wedding the way I want it. The bride is supposed to get what she wants, right? Well, this bride wants her sister. I sat down and called all the venues on our list one more time. It was my bridezilla moment."

Sophia couldn't help but laugh at Grace's pride in her supposed diva fit. "That's the sweetest bridezilla moment I've ever heard of."

"Seriously, Sophie, it's going to be one of the biggest

days of my life, and I need you there. I just can't imagine getting married without my sister as my maid of honor."

"Oh, Grace." The tears were instant, blurring her vision. The sugar slipped from her arm, but somehow Travis caught it before it made a spectacular five-pound splatter on the tile. She smiled up at him through her tears. "Thank you."

"You're welcome." He took the flour from her.

Sophia wasn't sure why Alex had invited Travis in for this little family moment, but she was glad he was here. He'd been there for her when she was upset that her sister didn't seem to need her, so it seemed right that he got to share this happy moment, too.

Now that Travis had freed Sophia's arms, she could hug Grace, precious Grace, the sister who still needed her. "I can't believe you're doing all of this just so I can be in your wedding. Thank you." She turned to Alex. "And thank you. You're okay with this?"

The way his expression softened when he looked at her sister made Sophia feel mushy inside.

"I wanted to marry her yesterday," he said. "I wanted to marry her the day before that, and the day before that. I'm very okay with this weekend instead of waiting for September. Very."

Sophia squeezed Grace's hands. "So you're doing this. What can I do? What about your dress? Do you want me to call in some favors? You look so good in Vuitton. I could ask them to overnight me some samples in white. I'll tell them it's for a big event. That's the truth, too. I'm sure we'll be photographed enough to make it worth their while."

Grace squeezed Sophia's hands in return. "I already had Mom's wedding gown taken out of storage and shipped here last month. It just needs cleaned and fluffed. The dress shop is going to detach the old crinoline and I'm going to wear a new one underneath, but they have that kind of thing in stock. It's not a problem at all."

"You're wearing Mom's wedding dress?"

Grace bit her lip. "I should have asked you. The crinoline is a minor alteration, I promise."

"You don't need my permission. I'm not your boss. It's as much your dress as mine."

"Yes, but is it okay with you?"

"You're going to be such a beautiful bride, you're going to make me cry, anyway, but this is really going to be unfair. I'm going to look like a blubbering mess in all your photos."

Because being with her sister felt like her old life, Sophia started brainstorming their usual plans. "We'll have to fly Tameka in to give me bulletproof makeup. If my nose turns red, I'll be in all the gossip rags as a coke addict or something. That's just what we need when I'm trying to let the controversy die down. We can fly in Jolin with Tameka. She does such great hair."

"No." Because this was not their old life, Grace interrupted. "I've already got a hairstylist here. Austin isn't exactly a backwater. My stylist is really good. The only person we're flying in from LA is you."

"Me?"

"It will look that way. We're going to sneak you off this ranch and fly you to the Dallas airport. You'll get a nice first-class seat from Dallas back to Austin. Everyone will text their friends that you're on their plane, and when you land here, the paparazzi will assume you flew in for the wedding. You, me and Kendry are going to set up base in a hotel suite, so that Alex doesn't see us before the big day."

Alex turned to Travis. "Which brings us to why I asked you to stop in. Texas Rescue, completely by coincidence, has decided to conduct a training exercise tomorrow. It involves extracting a practice patient by helicopter and transporting her to the Dallas airport's medevac facilities. We were wondering if we might be able to use this ranch as the starting point. It looks like you've got plenty of room for a helicopter to land around here somewhere."

As Travis and Alex worked out locations and timing for her escape, Sophia stood at the counter with Grace, pretending to be absorbed by their conversation. She really just wanted to look at Travis.

She reached into the brown paper grocery bag, and pulled out a random box. Instant oatmeal. That was fine.

But Travis, ah, Travis, he was more than fine, and he would be hers tonight.

Another box. Toothpaste. Fine.

She would have to make the memories of the coming night last for the next five days, though. The thought of not seeing Travis for nearly a week was hard. She'd just found him. Once she left for Austin—

"Sophia." Grace jerked Sophia out of her fantasy. She was shaking her head *no* as she pushed Sophia's hand back into the grocery bag.

"What is it?" Sophia looked into the bag. In her hand, she held the neat, rectangular box of a pregnancy test. She stared at it in horror; she'd almost taken it right out and set it on the counter.

"Why?" she whispered. "Why would you do this?"

Grace pulled her out of the kitchen with an artificial smile for Alex. "Girl stuff to talk about. Shoes for the dresses. Be back in a second."

Sophia yanked her arm free in the living room, the same room in which she'd stripped Travis just two short days ago, the room in which he'd stripped her. She wanted to stay that way, bared to him, unafraid to be her true self. He'd seen her tears and tantrums, her scars, her fears.

When she'd thought she was being terrible, he'd stood beside her and thrown tomatoes at the world. Dear God, he'd said it was easy to be nice to her. He'd kissed every inch of her body.

Now Grace had brought a pregnancy test into her kitchen.

"Why?" Sophia pleaded.

"You need to know, Sophie. You can't keep telling yourself maybe it was a bad test, maybe you'll get your period. Once you know for certain, you can decide what you want to do."

No! The word was stuck in her head. She didn't dare say it out loud; it would come out as a scream that echoed off the rafters of this great big lonely house.

Grace had it so wrong. Sophia would *not* get to decide what she wanted to do. Once she knew for certain, then she would have no choice but to deal with adoption agencies and obstetricians. She'd have to deal with Deezee in the worst possible way.

What she wanted to do was spend more time with Travis. That would no longer be an option, because what she would have to do was tell him she was pregnant by another man, and her time with him would be over.

She'd always known her time with him would be short. This wasn't her house. This wasn't her career. She could not hide here forever and go broke. But dear God, when she'd stripped herself bare in this room, she'd thought she'd have more than two days. She needed more than two days.

"Sophie?"

"July seventh." The words sounded polite, if stiff. They should have sounded like they'd been ripped from her soul. "I should get my period on the sixth or seventh. If I don't, I'll do the test."

Sophia forced herself to relax her shoulders, and tilt her

head just so, and let the tiniest bit of an encouraging smile reach her eyes. "So in the meantime, let's set that aside and focus on your wedding. I wouldn't want to have to tangle with Bridezilla Gracie. She sounds pretty fearsome."

Judging from the relieved hug Grace gave her, Sophia Jackson had just delivered another Oscar-worthy performance.

Chapter Sixteen

Sunset finally came.

The men left for the day—the young bachelors to crash in the bunkhouse, Clay to his own place off the ranch—and Travis experienced the piercing anticipation of having Sophia all to himself.

At the first sound of the barn door sliding open, he left his office and headed for her, his boots loud on the concrete, and he knew he had the arrogant smile of a man who knew he was minutes away from getting exactly what he wanted with the only woman he wanted it from.

"Sophia."

Her sneakers were silent and so was she, tackling him so that he caught her and they turned 180 degrees, his arms around her body, her hands in his hair, their mouths meeting. It was like this every night now, this first moment of pent-up desire that had to be released in a crashing kiss.

He set her back on her feet, but she began kissing her way from just under his jaw down his neck.

He loved it, but he had to ask. "Are we celebrating a good day or blowing off steam after a frustrating day?"

She shook her hair back. "So many emotions."

"The scene with your sister? That had to be a good emotion." He didn't know why she couldn't have made the wedding in September, but clearly, the coming weekend had worked out for everyone.

Sophia locked her hands together behind his waist, as he did to her. Hips pressed together, focused on one another, they talked among the disinterested horses. Travis enjoyed the prelude; Sophia wasn't the only one who looked forward to having someone to talk to every day.

"I thought my role in Grace's life was kind of over. I can't believe she wants me in her wedding that badly. Just as badly as I wanted to be there."

"I can. If you were my sister, you'd be my hero, too."

"Hero." She wrinkled her nose.

"You stepped in when your parents died. You saved the day when her life could've easily fallen apart. You achieved your own success at the same time, and pretty damned spectacularly. I started downloading the line-up of movies that you star in. I didn't realize there were so many."

"I wouldn't say I starred in them all, if any. Except for *Pioneer Woman*, most were just small parts. Supporting actress or ensemble work, at best."

He gave her a tug, pressing her more tightly against the hardness that was inevitable when she was in his arms. "It's impressive. You're a hero, but I thank the heavens every day that you are not my sister."

She deflected his praise. "I hope I didn't show how surprised I was when Alex came in the kitchen door with you. It was kind of fun to have to pretend we're just neighbors, or whatever we are. You were a very good actor, by the way."

"Poker face. I could hardly look at that blue tile countertop now that I know it is exactly the right height for—"

She stood on her toes and twined one leg around his. "For a midnight snack?"

He dropped that casual kiss on her lips, the one that a man could give a woman when he knew he had time with her. He took her hand to lead her to his office. "We need to talk about who knows you're here, though."

He sat in the desk chair, knowing she'd sit in his lap and drape an arm over his shoulder. She did, but she was frowning. "Who knows I'm here?"

"Just the MacDowells who signed the lease, and Grace and Alex. But someone else who is physically on the property should be aware, for days I'm not here. I want to let… I want…what are you doing?"

"I'm leaving tomorrow for five days. I want to stock up on my moments." She turned to straddle him.

He laughed a little until he realized she was serious. Her hand slipped in his back pocket for the protection he was now never without. She stood to wriggle out of her shorts. When she started to undo his jeans, he didn't object, not in the least, but there was an edginess about her tonight that wasn't familiar.

"There's a perfectly good bed about a hundred yards away from here," he said.

"I want you to think of me while I'm gone. Every time you sit in this chair, I want you to remember a special moment."

That didn't need an answer. It was obvious he'd never look at this chair the same way again. But there was that underlying edginess again, so he answered her anyway. "I'm never going to forget you, Sophia. Not one moment."

She looked at him, blue eyes filled with what he could

only call longing, and he wondered for the millionth time if this thing between them was really destined to end.

She closed her eyes and kissed him as she tore open the foil wrapper. With her hands, she sheathed him. With her body, she sheathed him again, and he was lost to any kind of further analysis except *yes* and *more*.

He unbuttoned her cotton shirt, exposing the inner curves of breasts shaped by pink lace. He kissed the precious freckle first, then tasted as much softness as he could through the lace. She rode him, making him shudder almost immediately with the need to maintain some semblance of control. With his hands, he tilted her hips to make sure she was making the contact she needed for her own satisfaction.

She put two fingertips on his forehead and pushed his head back against the chair, then grabbed his wrist and moved his hand to the arm of the chair. Leaning forward, pink lace so close to his face, she spoke into his ear. "Hey, Travis? Sit back and relax. I've got this."

She did. She definitely did.

He tried to take in the moment, tried to comprehend that this dream was real, so unbelievably, incredibly real. When they reached their completion, Sophia collapsed against him, her head on his shoulder. As her soft breath warmed his neck, he wrapped her tightly in his arms and savored this moment, too.

The tenderness stayed with him, every time. Sophia seemed to want it as much as she needed the physical release. She was a sex goddess who cuddled afterward. He was the man who appreciated just how irresistible that combination was.

It might be impossible to live without it.

She wriggled closer yet, keeping him inside her. His body felt thick and full, but sated—for now. It was clear to him that the hunger for her would never be satisfied for long.

"I can't believe I have to leave you for five days," she said. "I don't want to. Not when we've just discovered each other."

He kissed the top of her head. Twirled a strand of silver and gold around his index finger.

She pouted. "It's kind of like the honeymoon phase, you know? That's a rotten time to be apart. It's not like we're some old married couple and we've been together ten years or whatever. Then five days wouldn't be such a big deal."

Was she trying to convince herself that the power between them was just a novelty, a new toy they'd lose interest in someday? Surely an old boyfriend hadn't lost interest in her and looked for greener pastures somewhere else.

"Sophia Jackson, if you push me into a desk chair and straddle my lap ten years from now, you will get exactly the same response from me. Ten years from now, twenty years from now, I will never have had enough of you."

The moment was suddenly charged with tension instead of tenderness. He'd crossed a line. He'd said something he shouldn't have, not when she'd told him from the first that this thing between them was going nowhere. It certainly wasn't going ten years into the future.

He wouldn't take it back. It was true: he would want her forever. He brushed the lock of her hair across his lips, and let it go.

She picked up her head and sat up a little straighter, then smiled as if she didn't have a care in the world. "I'm looking forward to making more moments. We've got to stock up five days in one night. I hope you ate a big lunch."

It was cute. She was overlooking his serious statement, offering to get them back on track. It was her olive branch.

He accepted it. "We may have to build in a dinner break.

It will be more than five days. I spend a week with my family every Fourth of July."

Abruptly, the conversation was serious again. "You won't be here when I get back from the wedding?"

"Not for the rest of the week."

"No, you can't leave," she pleaded, startling him with her intensity.

He slid his hands up her ribs and gave her a reassuring squeeze. "I can't leave the ranch in May, but I do take time off. July is the slowest month for ranching. The calving's done, the weaning hasn't started. The cattle have plenty of natural grass to graze on. If I'm going to leave, this is the time to do it."

"You won't be here when I get back from the wedding? You'll be gone the rest of the week?"

"Right." He tried to soothe her with a smile. He offered his own olive branch, an easy way to keep things light. "But I'll make it up to you when I get back."

"Can you change your plans?"

The edginess was unmistakable, as if it were critical that he be available this week just so they could sneak into bed together after sunset. As if time were short, and this week in particular was all they had.

Something was so obviously wrong, dangerously wrong.

He held her more tightly. Her ribs expanded with each panicky breath between his palms.

"My family's expecting me. My mom, my grandparents, brothers, sisters. Most of us are in ranching one way or the other, so this is our big holiday get-together. Kind of like Christmas for the Chalmers family."

He shouldn't be able to speak so calmly. How could he explain the mundane routine of his life when the best thing to ever happen to him was literally about to slip from his grasp?

She put her hands on his shoulders, prepared to use him for leverage as she stood, but he stopped her, a reflexive grip to keep her from leaving.

Her fingers dug into his shoulders, as if she didn't want to leave, either. "When will you be back?"

"Sunday." He tried to make it sound as normal as it was.

"What date is that? July tenth? Eleventh? It's past the seventh, for sure."

"Something like that. I'd have to look at a calendar."

She said nothing, but misery was written all over her face.

"For God's sake, Sophia. Be up front with me. Is this your last week in Texas or something?"

"No, it's nothing. I hope. I don't know. I don't know what I'll be dealing with next week. This thing between us…"

She kept stopping, running out of words. He couldn't tell if she was angry or frustrated, nor if it was directed at him or at herself.

"What about this thing between us?"

"I knew it couldn't last long," she said defensively. "I told you there was no future in it."

"This thing." He was disgusted with the term. "You mean this connection. We are connected in every way we can be at this moment. So at this moment, you owe me, Sophia. What are your plans? What's happening after this week? You can't just disappear without a word."

She looked away. "I don't think I will."

"You 'don't think'? What kind of answer is that?"

He deserved more. They deserved more.

"I don't even know how long your lease is for." He was angry that he should have to fight for basic information from her. He released her abruptly, but she clutched him as if he was her lifesaver.

What was going on?

She set her forehead against his, pinning him in place with such an intimate motion. Their noses touched as she whispered. "I have the house until January, the whole time Mrs. MacDowell's on her mission trip."

"But? Talk to me, Sophia."

"I swear I don't know what's next, Travis. The future is really up in the air, but believe me that I'm not ready for this to end. I want to be here when you come back. I do."

He wanted to take all these intense, bewildering emotions and push them into passion, make love to her until they were reduced to what they understood, communication of the most basic needs. His body was growing hard inside her. He couldn't talk like this, and hunger be damned, they needed to talk.

He set her aside, stood and turned his back to her. Got rid of the condom. Tucked his shirt in. Prayed for... God knew what. Just a prayer: *please.*

Please, let me keep her a little longer. She was everything to him.

What was he to her? Someone she might leave, someone she might not?

He turned around. She stood in his ranch office in her sneakers and short-shorts, with her million-dollar hair and lovely features. She didn't look like anything else in his world. She had no connection to his life.

And yet this *thing*, this power, this connection between them existed whether it should or not.

He'd known from the beginning she wasn't going to stay. Knowing it and facilitating a helicopter to take her away were two different things.

He forced himself to ask the question. "Are you going back to LA? Since the wedding forced you out of hiding, are you done here?"

"We'll make it look like I'm flying back to LA, just like we're making it look like I'm living there now. Grace is basically inviting the paparazzi to find her wedding by making sure I'm seen flying in. All I can do in return is try to appease the paparazzi so they don't get too aggressive and ruin her big day. I've got to stop and answer when they shout questions at me, smile while they take photos. They'll tell me to 'look this way' or 'twirl around and show us your outfit,' and I'll have to do it so they'll go away."

She trailed her fingers over the computer keyboard on his desk. "It will help. They love a cooperative star. But it won't be enough to bury all the negative publicity I already generated, so I'll come back here after the wedding. I need to continue staying off their radar."

She flicked a glance his way. He was sure his relief showed. He felt like he could breathe again.

She pushed the space bar on his keyboard, but nothing happened. He'd powered the machine down for the day.

"Have you never typed 'Sophia Jackson' in your search bar, just to see what horrible things I did?"

He shook his head.

"You weren't tempted, even a little bit?"

"Braden told me enough."

"Oh. The ball. I don't think all those Texas Rescue people are going to be too thrilled to see me at the wedding. Alex is one of their doctors, you know. Half of the guest list volunteers for them. Maybe they'll give me a second chance to make a first impression." Her gaze drifted from the keyboard to the floor as she shrugged one shoulder. "Just kidding—I know it doesn't work that way."

Perhaps Sophia had brought it on herself, but Travis feared she was going to be very uncomfortable for her sister's sake. She was going to appease the paparazzi. She was going to spend a night with people who had reason to think badly of her.

There wasn't a thing he could do to erase Sophia's past. Not one thing, but he tried to offer her some encouragement. "Braden had less to say about you than about the guy that jumped on your table."

She looked up quickly at that. "You know about Deezee?"

"Braden said he stepped on his wife's dinner and gave you a crappy apology."

"That's as good a summary as any, I suppose." She gave a halfhearted chuckle.

"Do you think he'll show up again?" Travis had that restless feeling again, that need to keep an eye on her—but Texas was a big state, and he'd be almost three hundred miles away with his family on the wedding day.

"That was all orchestrated by his publicist. Deezee is too lazy to set anything up himself, so I doubt it."

Travis couldn't leave without making sure she had some kind of plan in place. "If he does, don't try to appease him. Don't try to calm him down or take him aside. If he wants attention, you won't be able to save your sister's wedding from his type."

"The only reason he'd be there would be because of me. I think I'd owe it to everyone to try to stop him."

"Let Alex handle it. It's his wedding, not yours. Jamie MacDowell's the best man, right? You're the maid of honor, so you should be near Jamie. And you know Braden."

"He kind of hates me."

"He doesn't. You'll be safe with the MacDowells. Quinn will probably be there, too."

"I take it Quinn is the third one in all the family portraits at the house. I'll only recognize him if he still has braces and a bad middle school haircut."

"I'm serious, Sophia. I don't want you trying to deal with this Deezee jerk."

For once, he wished the paparazzi had been right. He wished Grace had been setting up a wedding tent here on the ranch. He'd be here in September. He'd be here if Sophia got harassed. Hell, she wouldn't get harassed on his ranch in the first place. That was the point of her hiding here.

But now she was going to fly away, without him.

She acted like she didn't care, scoffing like she was some kind of tough street kid. "Deezee's got no game. It would just be a lot of noise. Same old, same old. While you're gone, you can log on to your favorite celebrity site and see if anything exciting happened. If it's really juicy, it might make TV. That would be a fun topic around your family dinner table. 'Look what this crazy chick who's staying on my ranch did.'"

He recognized the voice: she sounded like the woman in the thigh-high black boots, the one who said she didn't care when she cared so desperately. He knew her, and he loved her. It made him sick to think that he might have come home to find her gone to LA forever.

It would happen, sooner or later. In the meantime, he wanted to cherish her while he could, yet they were standing on opposite sides of a desk chair.

"I'm sorry, Sophia."

"For what? I'm the one who hooked up with a loser. But hey, I've helped countless people make a living off entertainment gossip as a result. It's all good."

That scoff. It was such an act. She couldn't hide her pain from him.

He sent the chair rolling and hugged her. She held herself stiffly, as if she didn't need affection. He held her as if they'd just finished another round of amazing sex in-

stead of a round of bad feelings and painful subjects, because she needed to skip right to the tenderness. So did he.

"I'm sorry you can't go anywhere without a camera in
your face. I'm sorry you need a place to hide in the first
place."

She made a small sound, a yip of pain like a hurt animal, and then she was hugging him back, burrowing into
him in that way she had.

He realized she was physically hiding. He wrapped his
arms around her more tightly, cupping the back of her head
with his hand, letting her hide her face behind his forearm.
He was grateful his life's work had given him the muscle
she could literally hide behind.

"You've got a safe place here. Go do your wedding and
get the paparazzi eating out of your hand. When you're
done, come back here, and be safe."

She took a shivery breath. "But you won't be here."

It wasn't just the sex, then. It wasn't even the friendship
and the camaraderie. She felt safer around him.

"I'll be back Sunday. Until then, Clay will know you're
here. You won't be alone."

She shook her head against the idea. "Don't tell Clay.
The more people who know about me, the less safe I am.
Grace and I learned that the hard way. It's been just me
and Grace for years."

"But now it's you and Grace and Alex and me, and
you're still safe. You could depend on Clay, too." He
stopped cupping her head and moved to lift her chin instead, wanting her to see that she had options. "You know
Jamie and his wife, Kendry. Count on them. Braden Mac-
Dowell and his wife. She's a doctor. She knows how to
keep someone's confidentiality. Quinn and his wife are
trustworthy."

"I've never trusted that many people. Ever."

"But you could. The ranch that owns the Appaloosa is just a few miles away, and the Waterson family is as solid as they come. When the paparazzi came calling, all I had to tell Luke was that the MacDowells had a houseguest, and he was there for me, no questions asked. You don't have to be so very alone, Sophia."

He let go of her chin to caress her face, not surprised his hand wasn't quite steady. He had too much emotion coursing through him. He loved her so damned much, and he wanted to give her this gift. "I'll build you a whole safety net here, baby. You can come here to stay."

She wanted it. He could see it in her expression as clear as day, but she didn't say yes. It hurt her not to say yes, but she didn't say it.

She raised her own unsteady hand to touch his face. "I love… I love that you care."

"I care."

"Did I ever tell you my secret fantasy about you?"

She was done with this moment of tenderness, then. It wasn't enough for Travis, but he was a patient man. He couldn't force Sophia to trust him any more than he could force a horse to trust him. Things took time. Things had to be earned.

For her, he would meet her on her terms. She wanted to talk fantasies.

"Does this fantasy have to do with more office furniture?" he asked.

But her smile was fleeting.

"In my fantasy, you take me on a date. We have a drink together at a place with a nice dance floor, and we talk while we have our first dance. By the second dance, maybe we stop talking, because it's so special to be moving in sync, and thinking this is a person you'd like to know better. You drive me home and say good-night, and you tell me you'd like to see me again. There are no cameras. No one calls me names on social media. No one runs a background check on you. No one cares at all, except the two of us, because we're the ones falling in love."

His heart squeezed so hard, he could only whisper her name.

"But it's a fantasy, you see, because that will never happen. This thing between us, it has no future, no matter how much I wish it did."

They had a future. He just didn't know what it looked like yet. But Sophia was afraid now, skittish and spooked, and he needed to be patient.

"We have this moment," she said.

He tried not to be spooked himself at the way she said the words, as if this could be their last moment.

"How would you like to spend it?" he asked.

"I want to make love to you all night and pretend that I don't have to leave for a wedding tomorrow."

"Then that's what we'll do."

He scooped her up as if she were the bride and carried her out of the barn.

Chapter Seventeen

Sophia was the weird one.

She stuck out like a sore thumb at the reception, and nobody wanted to talk to her. She'd thought she was lonely at the ranch during that first month, but she'd forgotten how lonely she could be when surrounded by people. She just didn't fit in.

It had started at the airport. The flight attendants had been so deferential, but she'd told herself they treated all the first-class passengers that way. Then the passengers had started holding their cell phones at slightly odd angles, and she'd known she was being photographed. *OMG. Look who is on my plane!*

She couldn't even go to the bathroom like a normal person. She had to practically clean the bathroom before she left, careful to make sure she left no drops of liquid soap or a crumpled paper towel that would mark her as a slob. *OMG. Sophia Jackson left the lid down on the toilet. Does that mean she went number two?*

The only time she'd been able to forget she was different than everyone else had been in the hotel, when it had been only her, Grace and Kendry MacDowell. Kendry had overcome that invisible distance between celebrity and fan pretty quickly, and they'd had such fun as co-conspirators, trying to make Grace laugh through her bridal jitters. If only there were more Kendry MacDowells in the world…

I'll build you a whole safety net here, baby.

Travis. That man was something special. That man deserved a good life with a good woman, not with an outcast like her.

OMG. Sophia Jackson is at this wedding reception. She eats only shrimp and strawberries. What a freak.

Sophia stood in no-man's land, somewhere between the bar and the band. It was too embarrassing to sit at the head table, because Grace and Alex were on the dance floor, as were Kendry and Jamie. The other groomsman, Kent, was a bachelor who'd been pulled onto the dance floor by a group of single women who weren't letting him go any time soon. Sophia couldn't sit at the table alone.

OMG. Sophia Jackson is like a total bitch. She won't speak to anyone.

She kept a pleasant, neutral smile on her face and watched her sister glow with happiness.

The wedding ceremony had been gorgeous, a traditional service in a white church. At one point it struck her that Kendry was standing next to her with a tiny life growing in her belly. What if she, Sophia, were doing the same? In the hush of the church, surrounded by flowers and lace, pregnant had seemed like an ultra-feminine, almost divine thing to be. Even if Sophia wasn't going to raise the baby herself, it was a miracle.

Would Travis see it that way?

It wasn't July seventh. She didn't have to worry about that yet. With luck, she'd never have to worry about that.

She glanced at the roof of an adjacent building. She'd been holding still too long. The cameraman had a clear angle to her. She moved to the other side of the bandstand.

"May I have this dance?"

Travis. The man behind her sounded just like Travis, and when she turned around, she saw that the handsome man in the suit and tie was Travis.

"It's you. Oh, it's so good to see you. I'm dying to hug you, but there are at least four telephoto lenses on us right this second from a roof and two balconies."

"I missed you, too. Would you care to dance?"

"That would be lovely, thank you."

The band was playing a slower song, the kind where the man and woman could hold each other in a civilized ballroom pose and sway together, even if it was their first dance. She really almost felt like crying, it was so perfect.

"I didn't know you were here," she said. "I didn't see you at the ceremony."

"I saw you. You looked radiant up there. Whatever you were thinking, it looked good on your face."

This was their first dance, but they weren't strangers. Sophia lowered her voice. "I may have been thinking about you and a certain desk chair?"

"I don't think so."

"You and a kitchen counter?"

"Wrong again."

Oh, this was wonderful, to dance and flirt and feel like she belonged at the party. "How do you know what I was thinking?"

"Because I know the look on your face when you think of countertops and chairs, and that wasn't it. Probably a good thing when you're standing in a church."

It was wonderful to be with Travis, who knew her and didn't ask about filming *Space Maze* or whether she'd done her own stunts in *Pioneer Woman*.

"So what do you think I was thinking?"

"You were probably thinking about the child you helped raise, and how she's turned into a lovely woman. Grace is a beautiful bride. You must be very proud of her. I'm very proud of you."

Sophia felt her happiness dim. She had been thinking about a child, but it was one that, if it existed, would end this fantasy with Travis sooner rather than later.

"Grace was a teenager when I took over, not a child."

"You need to learn how to take a compliment. For example, you look very beautiful all dressed up. I've only ever seen you in yoga clothes and shorts. And one pair of thigh-high black boots. What did you do with those boots, by the way?"

She smiled. "I didn't know you owned a suit. It's kind of surreal to see you away from the ranch."

"Now that is exactly how not to return a compliment. I think you're very intriguing, though. Can I get you a drink?"

That's when it hit her. "Travis Chalmers. You're giving me my fantasy, aren't you?"

But he'd already turned to introduce her to a man he knew. Then a woman. He got the conversation onto a topic that everyone found interesting, and then he melted into the crowd. She hated to see him go, but she knew it would save anyone from guessing they were a couple.

She danced with some of the men she talked to. Then Travis returned for a second dance, as she'd known he would. A drink, two dances, an invitation to go out again: the fantasy she had said would never come true.

They swayed in silence this time, not just because that

had been her fantasy, but because her heart was too full to speak for at least two verses and a chorus.

"This isn't just about my fantasy, is it? You came to make sure that the Texas Rescue people gave me a second chance."

"I think they like you. God knows the men are happy enough to dance with you. They just needed to see me do it first, so they'd know you were a mortal even though you look like a goddess. Beauty can intimidate people."

Tears stung her eyes. That hadn't felt like a compliment as much as a benediction. Travis believed in her. She didn't want to be the weird one, even if it meant she was the beautiful weird one, and he understood that.

"Clay is going to call you to tell you if I make it home safely, isn't he?"

"Yes, he knows you're living in the house now. I told you that I would do anything to help you whether you liked it or not. Telling Clay was one of those things. I couldn't leave you isolated in hiding. Anything could happen, even a house fire, and no one would have known you were there. It wasn't safe. Clay knows, and only Clay knows."

Subdued, humbled, she asked, "Where's Deezee?"

"He's working at a club in Las Vegas tonight. You won't be embarrassed by him, and your sister has already forgotten he exists."

I love you.

She wanted to say it, she was dying to say it, but Deezee did exist, and her sister wouldn't be the only one reminded of it if July seventh turned out the way Sophia feared.

"I'd like to see you again, Sophia. I'll be out of town for the rest of the week, but could I take you to dinner on Sunday? There's a place just outside of Austin that I think you'd enjoy."

She tried to play her role. "Really? Where?"

"My house. Genuine Texas cuisine."

She wrinkled her nose. "Zucchini and tomatoes?"

"Steak and a baked potato. Dress is casual. I'll pick you up at eight."

Her voice was thick with tears as the song and her fantasy ended. "I'll see you on Sunday. Have a nice visit with your family."

By Sunday, she would know one way or the other. Either she'd tell Travis she loved him, or she'd tell him she was pregnant with another man's child.

They had to part without a kiss.

Sophia wondered if she'd ever get a chance to kiss him again.

July sixth came and went without any hoopla. Sophia talked to Clay a bit and to Samson a lot.

The seventh came and went as well. Sophia tried throwing a few tomatoes, but it was too lonely without Travis leaning on a pillar, evaluating her technique. Instead, she breathed in the shimmering hot air as she poked around the front yard until she found the goose salt shaker, dirty but unbroken. She took it into the house and scrubbed it until there was no trace of evidence that Sophia had once pitched it into the night sky.

On the eighth, she had to do the pregnancy test. She'd promised. She intended to, but she felt that need to hibernate. She slept most of the day, and by the time evening fell, she thought it would be best to wait until morning. She'd gone back to Mrs. MacDowell's 1980s pregnancy handbook and flipped through the opening pages gingerly, with one finger. There seemed to be something magical about the first urine of the day. So really, she might as well go to bed and do the test first thing in the morning.

On the morning of the ninth, she took the test. She could no longer fool herself: she was pregnant.

She cried the entire day.

The movies had gotten it all wrong. The end of the world was not an isolated, brown landscape.

Sophia woke to summer sunshine pouring in her bedroom window, mixing with the bluebonnet paintings on the walls. It was beautiful.

But it was Sunday.

Travis was coming back, and at eight in the evening, he'd pick her up to take her back to his house for dinner. There, she was going to tell him that she was pregnant with another man's child, that she'd been pregnant all along but too stubborn and willful to admit it to herself, and because of that, she'd sucked him into a hopeless situation.

It was the end of the world.

Black seemed like the appropriate color. Sophia dressed in black yoga clothes, tied on her sneakers, and went to visit the horses.

As always, Samson liked her best. She leaned on his great, warm neck and wished someone would yell *cut*.

The barn door slid open. After five days back in the public eye in Austin, that old reflex to keep her appearance together had returned. She stood properly, shoulders back and down, ankles together, hand on hip—but with her other hand, she tickled Samson under his chin. She hoped it was only Clay coming back for something he'd forgotten. No matter what Travis said, she didn't want more people knowing she was hiding on the ranch.

"Now, this is a fantasy."

"Travis." She drank in the sight of him as he stood just inside the barn door. He looked so achingly good, as if she hadn't seen him for a year instead of a week. Less than that, since he'd surprised her at her sister's wedding.

"To see a woman as beautiful as you are hanging out in cute shorts, talking to my horses, well, you just know that's some rancher's fantasy. Luckily, I'm a rancher."

She wanted to run and throw herself in his arms the way she always did, spinning him halfway around with the impact.

But she was pregnant. She held still.

Travis had no hesitation. He strode toward her, single-minded, confident. He scooped her up and spun her around, bringing enough momentum for the two of them.

His arms felt so strong. He smelled so good. Somehow, she'd been so focused on how they were going to be apart, it was startling to have him here—and still so happy with her.

Because he didn't know. Not yet.

"I didn't think I'd see you until dinner." How could her voice sound so normal when she was dying inside?

"I missed you," he said.

"I missed you, too." It was true. Surely she was allowed to say that.

He linked his arms around her waist, the way they did when they settled in to catch up on how their days had gone. Had he missed just talking to her? She thought her heart might burst.

"I watched a couple of your movies because I missed you so much."

She was grateful to talk about anything except what she needed to talk about. "Which ones?"

He named the crime drama, the one with the smoking-hot sex scene.

"Oh. That one." She felt her cheeks warm as she looked toward the tack room. She couldn't hold his gaze.

"I want credit for keeping my eyes on yours and not letting them drop lower, but if you don't look at me, how will you know how good I am at pretending I'm not thinking about your body?"

He sounded amused.

She looked at him then. "That scene doesn't bother you? I mean, knowing anyone could watch it?" She knew so many fellow actors whose significant others were bothered greatly by those kinds of scenes, even when carefully arranged bedsheets protected privacy. Her costar's girlfriend had been standing by as they filmed that one, anxious and jealous and making the role ten times harder to play. She'd been far more of a diva than any actress Sophia had worked with.

Travis kept his arms locked around her waist. "I've seen rated R movies my entire adult life without thinking twice about it, but it is strange when you know one of the actors. It took a few scenes for me to adjust to hearing you speak with a Boston accent. If you're worried about the sex scene, don't be. I could tell it wasn't real."

"Oh, it's not. It's really not. There are a dozen people working, and you have to hold yourself in the most unnatural way, and there was this awful bubblegum smell, and I remember being thirsty and worried about how to deliver this line that I didn't think my character would really say, and they put makeup on everything. I mean everything."

"I know."

"You do?"

In the moment of silence that followed, she forgot they had no future. She could only think how lucky she'd be to have such an even-tempered man as her partner in life.

"How?" she asked, holding her breath.

"It didn't look real to me. Not the look on your face,

which was sexy as hell, don't get me wrong, but it wasn't what you really look like with me."

"Oh."

He kissed her lightly. "You look sexier with me."

"Oh."

"I could guess about the makeup because your freckle was missing. The one that's right here." Without taking his eyes from hers, he placed his finger precisely on a spot just above the edge of her bra, on her left breast, exactly where she knew she had a little black dot.

"Oh. They hide that all the time, even if I'm just wearing a low cut gown or a bathing suit."

His grin slowly grew into a smile. "Good. I love it. I'll keep it to myself. The audience doesn't get the same you that I get."

She wanted to smile back, but she was dying inside. *We have no future. We have no future.*

"The movie I'll never watch again was the pioneer one," he said.

"That was my best. Everyone says so." The words came out by rote despite her frantic thoughts.

"You died. I don't ever want to know if that looked realistic. I can't watch that one again."

He kissed her as if he couldn't bear to lose her, and she kissed him back the same way. *No future, no future.*

She would lose him, soon, but she wasn't ready to say the words. She was supposed to have had until eight o'clock to prepare herself to say the words.

"Why are you here? I mean, why did you leave your family so early for me?"

"That was why—for you. I couldn't wait until tonight to see you. I just gave Clay the rest of the day off. I realize your fantasy includes a very traditional dinner that might end in a peck on the cheek, but I was going to try to persuade you to try a different fantasy now."

Her body was her traitor in every way. She knew she couldn't sleep with Travis again, but her body didn't care, pregnant or not. Just being near him was enough to make her come awake and alive once more.

Patch saved the day. With outstanding timing, she ran into the barn to greet Travis as if he'd been gone ten years.

Sophia stepped back to give the dog room. She pretended she didn't see the quizzical look Travis threw her.

"How're you doing, Patch?" He bent down to pet her with both hands. There was something odd about the way he did it, almost like he was checking something, deliberately feeling his way from the dog's shoulders to her tail. "Still feeling good, girl?"

Sophia grasped at the distraction. "Is there something wrong with her?"

Travis stood again. "I wouldn't say it's wrong. She's going to have puppies. Judging from the amount of time she's been spending in Samson's stall, she's planning on having them there. I'll have to move Samson when she gets a little closer. They're best friends, but I wouldn't want him to step on a puppy."

Sophia felt her stomach tying itself into knots. "I can't take another abandoned animal crying from starvation. Is there replacer milk for puppies? Do you have any? We should get some right away. Right away."

She must have overreacted. Travis's quizzical look deepened into concern. "Patch is a good mother. This is her second litter, so I don't anticipate any problems, but sure, we'll keep some replacer milk here. I won't leave you with a starving newborn again, I promise."

He kissed her again, not on the lips, but on the forehead. She told herself that was for the best. It was already starting, this transition from lovers to friends that she was going to rely on. She'd had time, too much time, to think about her options, and no matter what Grace had said, there weren't many.

Sophia had nowhere else to hide. She was going to have to stay on this ranch for the duration of her pregnancy, and that meant she was going to see Travis. Staying on good terms with him was essential, because frankly, she was scared to death to be without him.

She had a good speech she needed to be ready to deliver tonight that talked about how they'd be able to coexist quite nicely together despite their history. It left out the part about being scared.

Until tonight's dinner, she needed to not freak out. She smiled brightly at Travis. "First the cat, now the dog. Is everything on this ranch pregnant?"

Travis kept looking at her, but she told herself he was smiling indulgently. "We try to keep it that way."

She tossed her hair, praying for normalcy. "You know that sounds terrible, right?"

"That's the ranching business. We had a ninety-seven-percent pregnancy rate in the cattle last year. That's a very good year. But I don't breed cats. She did that on her own. And I suspect Patch here found herself a boyfriend over at the James Hill."

"If she'd been neutered, then you wouldn't have this problem." She couldn't quite keep her tone light. She'd said the same thing after the cat. She'd thought the same thing about herself.

"I wouldn't say Patch having puppies is a problem. She's the fourth or fifth generation of River Mack cow dogs. She's got real good instincts, passed down through her line. People in these parts are glad to have one of her puppies. This will be her second litter, though, so we'll have her fixed. I don't want her to get worn out. I need her working the herd this fall."

"What happens this fall?"

He was silent for a long time. Then he walked up close to her and, as if she were some kind of precious treasure, held her head gently in his hands and rested his forehead on hers.

"The last time we were together before the wedding we talked just like this. You weren't sure if you'd still be on the ranch this week. You said you'd have a better idea of what the future holds when I came back. I'm back. Do you know? Are you going to be here this fall?"

It was hard, so hard, not to dive into the safety of his arms. He'd hold her close and she'd feel safe and everything would be all right.

Those days were over. Those days never should have been, so she stayed on her own two feet and answered him honestly. "Yes, I'll be here all the way until January."

As close as they were, she could feel the relief pass through his body, but she could see his frown of worry as well. She wasn't a good enough actor to fool him. He knew she was holding something back, but being Travis, he didn't push.

"Well, then," he said. "Would you like to see what the ranch looks like beyond the house and barn? It's a Sunday in July. There won't be a soul for miles around. I'll drive you around and tell you what you can expect from now until Christmas."

And tonight, I'll tell you what to expect.

But she was being offered a reprieve, a stay of execution, and she loved him too much to deny herself his company, just one more time.

Chapter Eighteen

"I didn't realize there were so many flowers."

Sophia looked out the window of the white pickup truck. She was all buckled in, huddled by the door, and sad. The ranch had so much beauty, and she'd missed it all when she'd first arrived.

"What did you think it was if it wasn't flowers?"

"Brown. I just thought I was coming to live in exile on some ugly brown planet. But it's flowers. Yellow, purple and orange." She felt a little defensive. The old Sophia was just so pitiful. "You put those colors together, and you get brown."

"Until you take a closer look. Which you are."

She closed her eyes against his kindness. Of course she was in love with this man. How could she not be in love with this man? And he was going to hate her so very soon.

"Stop being so nice to me."

He drove in silence for another little while. "Why are you finding it so hard to be nice to yourself?"

She didn't answer him. Out the window, there were babies everywhere. Quite literally, every single cow had a calf suckling or sleeping underfoot. She could see the satisfaction and pride in Travis's expression—or she had seen it, before her misery had spilled into the pickup.

Travis slowed down the truck and squinted at a distant tree. "There she is. It's about time."

He parked the truck a little distance from the tree and got out. There was a cow under the tree, sleeping peacefully on her side. "You can come out if you want. Just be quiet about slamming the door."

Travis walked a little closer to the cow, not too close, and then crouched down. He checked his watch. And he waited.

And waited.

The minutes ticked by, until Sophia couldn't stand it anymore. She got out of the truck and practically tiptoed up to Travis before dropping down beside him.

"What's going on?"

"She's the last heifer of the season, and by season, I mean she's so far out of season, she's in a class by herself."

"I don't understand."

Travis checked his watch again as the cow huffed and made a halfhearted attempt to get up. The cow fell still again.

"We have our calving season in April and early May on the River Mack. That's when we want the herd giving birth."

"All at the same time?"

"More or less. You have to ride the herd several times a day, looking for new babies to doctor, making sure the mamas are on their feet and nursing, and sometimes—" he stood up with a sigh "—you have to pull a calf."

He walked back to the truck, dug around the back, and

returned with some blue nylon straps and a pair of long, skinny plastic bags. "This little lady tricked us pretty well. We thought she was pregnant during breeding, but turns out she wasn't. Then a bull jumped a fence, and here she is, totally out of sync with the rest of the herd. Accidents happen, though."

The cow moaned again. Travis shook his head.

"What's wrong?" Sophia stayed crouched on the ground, her fingertips on the grass for balance.

"She's a first-time mother. She isn't doing too well. She must have been at this awhile. See how tired she is?"

And then Travis walked right up to the laboring cow. Sophia stood to see better. There were two front legs poking out of the mother's…body. Legs with hooves and everything. Sophia cringed.

The mother seemed to get agitated as Travis stood there, but then the hooves poked out a little farther and the nose of a cow came out, too. Travis came back and crouched beside Sophia.

Nothing else happened for an eternity. He checked his watch and picked up the blue straps again, but then the cow made a pitiful sound of pain and the whole head of a tiny cow came out with its front legs.

"There you go," Travis said under his breath.

Sophia sat on her butt. "I'm gonna be sick."

He turned his head to look at her. "You've never seen anything being born?"

"No." She couldn't look. "What are the blue straps for?"

He seemed amused, which, given that he was in full cowboy mode, meant one corner of his mouth lifted in barely-a-grin. "You can wrap 'em around the calf's legs and help the mama out. It's called pulling a calf."

"You're kidding me. This is what you do all day? I

thought you rode around on a horse and shot rattlesnakes or something."

He turned back to the laboring cow. "I do that, too. These mamas go to a lot of trouble to have their babies. It's the least I can do to make sure the babies don't get bit by something poisonous."

He would be the best father in the world.

The thought hit her hard, followed equally hard by sorrow at the memory of Deezee. She'd been so unwise, so very unwise.

But then the cow moaned and the entire calf came out in a rush of blood and liquid. It just lay there, covered with gunk, and Sophia's heart started to pound. The world got a little tilted. She grabbed Travis's arm, digging her fingers into his muscle to keep herself vertical.

"Come on, Mama," he said quietly.

The mother wasn't moving. The baby wasn't moving.

Then Travis was moving, on his feet and heading toward them as he pulled the plastic bags over his hands and arms—they were gloves. He grabbed the baby's nose, its lifeless head bobbling as he jerked some kind of membrane from around it. Then he grabbed the hooves in his hands and simply dragged the calf out of the puddle of grossness and across the grass to plop it right in front of the mother's face.

This was birth. This horrible, frightening death and membranes and pain—*oh, my God.* Sophia rolled to her hands and knees and tried desperately not to vomit.

What had she been thinking? That she'd do yoga and eat well and sport a small baby bump? Maybe toward the end, around Christmas, she'd be a little bit roly-poly for a few weeks, but then the baby would be born and go off to some wonderful adoptive family and everything would be clean and neat and tidy. She'd move on with her life.

That wasn't how it was. She had to give birth, she had to *labor*, there was just no way out of it. There would be gushing yuck and pain and exhaustion. And if, at the end of it all, the poor little baby didn't move…

What if the poor little baby didn't move?

She dug her fingers into the dirt and panted.

"Sophia."

She was dimly aware that Travis had come back. She heard him cursing, saw bloody plastic gloves being dumped on the grass. His clean arm was strong around her waist as he picked her up and set her on her feet, but he kept her back to his chest, which was smart because she was about to throw up.

"Baby, it's okay. Look, the mama's taking care of her calf now. She was just too tired to get up and go do it, so I helped her out. It's okay."

"No, it is *not*!" She wrenched free from him and ran a few steps toward the truck, but there was really nowhere to go. "I don't want to do it. I don't want to."

"Do what?"

"You're a man." Her words were getting high-pitched, rushing together. "Would you want to go through that? It's awful. She could've died. That baby could've died. I don't want to do it."

"It's okay. You don't have to do anything." He captured her in his arms again and tried to soothe her, making little shushing noises like she was the baby.

She started to cry. "Yes, I do. I'm the woman."

She could feel him behind her, shaking his head like he was dumbfounded, but how could he be? He was the one who'd just gotten out straps and gloves. "Okay, you're a woman, but you're just spooking yourself. You're not going to give birth anytime soon."

She was crying so hard now, she was doubled over at

the waist. She would have fallen if Travis didn't have his arm around her. "Yes, I am. I have to. I'm pregnant."

Travis was an ass for the next seven weeks.

For the first few minutes, he'd held Sophia as she'd choked and cried, although it was frankly a toss-up which one of them was more staggered.

Pregnant. They'd been careful, except for that very first time. He'd only been inside her for a minute, and he hadn't climaxed—but it was possible. That could be all it took, as they'd been warned in sex ed pamphlets given to them a hundred years ago at school. He'd assumed he was the father.

It would be nice to be able to claim that he'd felt some noble calling or had a divine moment of parenthood fall upon his shoulders at the news that Sophia was pregnant, but in fact he'd been trying to hold a woman who was about to vomit, and he'd been doing math. June plus nine months.

"March?" That had been his first brilliant contribution to her distress.

"January," Sophia had gasped, and his world had gone to hell.

His horse tossed his head. Travis was holding onto the reins too tightly. Again. He tried to relax in the saddle, but it was damned hard when he was getting closer to the house. He hadn't caught a glimpse of Sophia in seven weeks, but that didn't stop him from looking.

The rest of July had been a haze of hurt feelings. One of the reasons she'd come to the ranch in the first place was to hide her pregnancy once she got bigger. *She should have told me. Her sister should have told me. Her brother-in-law should have told me.*

He hadn't questioned that assumption in July, but it was the first week of September now, and he did. Why should they have told him? He was a stranger to them. How did he think that first day should have gone? Grace and Alex, standing by their open car doors, should have said what, exactly? *Are you the foreman? This is our sister, Sophia. She's pregnant.*

August had been hot and slow on the ranch. Travis had only ridden half days as he watched the cow-calf pairs thrive on summer grass. The indignation had changed to something else. *If only she'd told me at the beginning. If only her sister had told me. If only I'd known...*

But it was September now, and he realized he'd never finished the thought.

If only she'd told him at the beginning, *then what?*

DJ Deezee Kalm would still be the father. The week of the wedding, Travis had verified Deezee's schedule to make sure he'd keep away from Sophia and her sister. *If only I'd known...*

He still would have kept Deezee away from Sophia. The man was still a jerk. He'd still made life hard for Sophia in more ways than leaving her pregnant and alone. He'd hurt her career, her income, her self-confidence.

Sophia was planning on giving the baby up for adoption. Travis had been incredulous when she'd told him so on that awful day. His whole life was spent watching mothers rear their young. He couldn't imagine Sophia not wanting to rear hers, but now he wondered what kind of influence Deezee might have been on that decision.

Travis had that impatient feeling again. He needed to lay eyes on Sophia. Seven weeks was far too long.

He let his horse walk faster. The house wasn't far away now. He knew the terrain like the back of his hand. Down this slope, up the next rise, and he'd see the white pillars.

The old lie came to him as easily as it had so many

times before. If he could just check on Sophia, then he'd be able to put his mind at rest and move on.

A gunshot rang out.

In an instant, Travis's thoughts crystallized: the only thing in his world that mattered was Sophia.

She was in danger.

Chapter Nineteen

"Damn, girl. You look like a pregnant cow."

Sophia didn't bother to answer Deezee. She was twenty-one weeks along, halfway through her pregnancy, so of course she had a baby bump. She still wasn't wearing maternity clothes. Her stretchy yoga top covered her fine. Obviously, Deezee had never seen a pregnant cow if he thought she resembled one.

Deezee shut the door to his car, a black luxury sedan. He wasn't driving it, though. That privilege belonged to one of his ever-present buddies. Sophia didn't recognize this particular buddy. The back doors opened and two more men came out.

Afraid to be alone with your own thoughts, Deezee? Still?

But she wouldn't say anything out loud. She'd been expecting her lawyer, the one who was supposed to arrive first with the adoption papers for Deezee to sign with her.

She'd texted Clay that a black sedan would be coming onto the property today, so it had come through all three gates unchallenged, she was sure. She'd never expected Deezee to arrive in such a traditional car.

Her little burner phone could only text and call, but it couldn't do either of those things right now, because it was in the house, and she was on the patio. If she made a run for the door, she had no doubt someone from Deezee's crew would get there before she had the door closed and locked behind herself. She didn't want to be locked in the house with these guys.

None of Travis's men would be coming to check on her. And Travis himself? He wasn't speaking to her. She'd never seen a man as shocked as he'd been when she'd told him the baby wasn't his.

Clay was her only point of contact at the ranch now, and she'd told him she wanted the black sedan to come to the house. Round and round, back to the beginning: Sophia was stuck for the next ninety minutes with Deezee and his posse.

A little shiver of fear went down her back.

"You're early," she said, then immediately wished she hadn't. They were almost three hours early. The lawyer had arranged it so that he'd be here long before they were, and Deezee was never early to anything, until today.

"No prob, girl. Let's check out the new place. What do you have to drink?"

She was an actor. She needed to pull this role off. "I don't have anything you like. I'm pregnant, so...no alcohol." She held up her hands and shrugged. "I think if you go back to the main road and head west, the very next road takes you to a local bar. That might be fun. The lawyer won't be here with the paperwork for another hour, anyway. Might as well go do some shots."

One of the backseat buddies liked the idea. *Please, please, please talk your gang into going.* Of course, the next road to the west didn't lead to a bar. It led to the Watersons' ranch, but Deezee would probably drive a good half mile in before he realized it. Maybe the Watersons would detain them.

Travis trusted the Watersons. They would've been part of her safety net, if she'd been smart enough to accept it. She hoped the Watersons would forgive her for sending Deezee onto their property, but if they were friends of Travis, it was her best bet for safety.

"Let's go," the backseat buddy said, enthusiastic to find the bar.

Hope swelled in Sophia's chest.

"Nah-nah-no-no-no." Deezee waved off his buddy with a shake of his blinged-out fingers.

Hope burst like a bubble.

"I gotta check this place out. We are in the *sticks*. Damn, girl, whatchu do out here all alone?"

I cry.

She smiled. "Well, like you said, you've now checked the place out. This is all there is." She snapped her fingers. "You know where there might be some beer? In the bunkhouse. Just go past this barn and follow that fence. You can't miss it."

She knew exactly how the hands who had the day off would react to these four storming into the bunkhouse. *Please, Deezee, go get some beer from the bunkhouse.*

"Why are you so anxious to get rid of me?"

Sophia had not done her best acting. She was nervous. She'd never felt so vulnerable, and Deezee could see it.

"Don't you want to party anymore?" he asked. "Oh, yeah. You got a bun in the oven." He turned to his friends.

"How about that, boys? I'm not shooting blanks. Who knocked up Sophia Jackson? This guy."

The gunshot took her completely by surprise. She jumped a mile. Even Deezee dropped the f-bomb on his friend for the deafening sound.

The man had pulled out a handgun and was aiming it at the barn. "Just testing out the 'you can't hit the broad side of a barn' thing." He fired again. "My father used to say that. I hated my father."

"Stop!" Sophia ran from the patio toward him. "There are horses in there. Dogs. Cats. You'll hurt something."

She grabbed his arm, but he shook her off and fired again.

"Please," she begged. "It's a real barn. You'll kill something."

"Give me that." Deezee held out his hand for the gun. He took more careful aim than his friend. "Calling the shot. Eight ball in the corner pocket."

"*Stop!*" Sophia yelled, lunging for his arm before the sound of pounding horse's hooves could register in her head.

Travis was there, off his horse while it was still galloping. He shoved Deezee's arm down. The gun fired into the dirt, then he twisted it from Deezee's grip. Travis ejected the magazine, cleared the chambered round, and then threw the empty gun as far as an outfielder to first base.

"Sophia, get in the house."

Deezee adopted all the arrogant posture he was capable of, but he backed up a step. "Who do you think you are, ordering my wife around?" He turned to the driver. "Show him the marriage license."

Sophia blinked as Travis decked her alleged husband.

Deezee was out.

"What the eff, man?" the driver said to Travis. "You planning on taking on all three of us now?"

"Yes."

None of the three made a move against him.

"Sophia, get in the house." Travis repeated the order through gritted teeth.

She wanted to stay by Travis's side, but she felt the baby kick. This wasn't just about her safety, so she ran for the kitchen door as more men from the River Mack came thundering up the road.

"I want to go check on the puppies."

"Sophia, please, try to relax. Buck said the animals are all fine. Are you uncomfortable?"

She was lying on the couch with her upper body in Travis's lap and his arm supporting her neck and shoulders. His other hand hadn't stopped smoothing over her hair, her shoulder…her belly. She hadn't been this comfortable since the last time they'd made love.

"I'm fine. How are you? You're the one who had the fistfight."

"You're the one who's pregnant. My God, Sophia…" He cradled her closer for a moment, then put his head back and sighed.

"I'm okay, really." Her heart felt more and more okay each time he did that. "I never threw a punch."

"You didn't have to throw a punch to have all your muscles pumped full of adrenaline. I can feel that my muscles are worn-out from the tension, and yours are way more important than mine right now." His hand smoothed its way over her belly again.

"Thank you."

He was silent.

"Thank you for treating me right, and for coming to my rescue, and for being an all-around decent man."

"I've been an ass. You should be kicking mine instead of apologizing to me. I love you, Sophia. I have from the very first, and I could kick myself for wasting the entire month of August feeling sorry for myself."

"Well, it's kind of a big deal to find out your lover is carrying another man's child. Don't say it isn't."

His hand drifted over her hair again, petting her, soothing her. Loving her. "Okay, let's get this settled. It's a big deal, I agree. But I could have talked to you about it. I could have asked you my questions, instead of asking myself questions over and over that I couldn't possibly know the answer to."

"I know I should—"

"There's more."

He looked so fierce, Sophia's heart tripped a little.

"I apologize for taking so long to realize the obvious. I kept saying to myself, 'if only I'd known,' until I finally realized it wouldn't have mattered. What if I'd known you were pregnant when you first arrived here? I would have found you fascinating, anyway. What if you'd had this cute baby bump when you were throwing those tomatoes? We still would've ripped off our clothes in the living room."

"Travis—"

"What if you'd arrived here with a newborn baby? I still would have fallen in love with you. The key is you, Sophia. I will always love you."

"I'm—I'm—" She gave up and snuggled into his chest, because he was big and strong and she could. "I'm going to live on that forever. That fills my heart up."

He kissed her, which was exactly what she wanted.

"Aren't you angry with me at all?" he whispered over her lips.

"No. I watch you through the window every day. You've looked so grim, and I've known it was because of me. I'm so sorry."

She didn't want him to think the worst of her. "I know this sounds hard to believe, but I really was in denial. I read that the pregnancy test could be false positive, and my brain just seized on that as the right explanation, because it was the only explanation I could handle. My career wouldn't be impacted. I wouldn't be tied to Deezee in any way. You came later, but once I met you, that was all the more reason to just ignore the possibility. I sound like an idiot, don't I?"

"There's nothing about you that sounds like an idiot." He kissed her sweetly, casually, like he had hours to kiss her whenever he pleased. "I'm sleeping here tonight. It's going to be a while before I can let you out of my sight. That's not too rational, either."

"I like that, though. You know you won't be sleeping with a married woman, right? I really want you to know I'm not in denial about that. Deezee is just trying to stir up gossip with that paperwork."

"I know. I'm glad the lawyer is releasing a statement for you."

The lawyer had shown up punctually, only to find himself being asked to clarify all kinds of points of law beyond adoption. A quick internet search had cleared up the alleged St. Barth's marriage certificate. Thirty days' notice was a minimum requirement to marry on that island, and they'd only flown in for the weekend.

More importantly in Sophia's mind, she'd never said *I do*. Deezee's antics at the altar had been her last straw. She'd thrown her bouquet at him when she was only halfway down the aisle, something that had made her look terrible in photos, but it had been her one justifiable tantrum.

She pulled far enough away from Travis to look at him directly. "I'm not married, and I've never been married."

He studied her for a moment. "Are you thinking of my dad?"

"Maybe. Yes. I know you don't admire what he did. I think you would never sleep with a married woman."

He brushed her hair back from her eyes. "If I had to wait for your divorce to be final, I would. After meeting Deezee, there's no way I would want you to stay married to him. Am I grateful that we don't need to wait for a divorce?" He laughed to lighten the moment. "That's like asking me if the sky's blue."

Sophia wished she could smile back. "You must question my judgment for even thinking about marrying him. I do. Grace hated him from the first, but he wasn't always quite so bad. He started using the drugs they sold at his raves. Then he started using even when there wasn't a party on. It got pretty out of control before I left him. It's magnified every flaw a hundred times."

"Sophia?"

"Yes?"

"I don't care about Deezee. You are an amazing woman no matter who you used to date."

Sophia placed her hand on her belly.

She cared. And she was scared.

Chapter Twenty

"I've got an early Christmas gift for you."

"Seriously?" Sophia asked. Travis thought she sounded equal parts excited and skeptical as she dumped the last scoop of oats into the trough in the mare's stall. "Wasn't a house enough?"

She'd fallen in love with the century-old foreman's house. She loved that it had a little parlor and a library and a dining room instead of one expansive space—so Travis had bought it for her. The MacDowells sold it to him along with a dozen acres or so, just enough land to make a nice little residential property along the edge of the River Mack. The renovations, including the baby's room, would be finished by the end of January, when Sophia's lease was up.

Until then, he would continue to live with her in the main house. Never again would he go seven weeks without seeing her. Sophia's next movie would begin shooting in July, and her new manager had added contract riders to keep the future Chalmers family together. Sophia's housing on location would accommodate the baby and a nanny, and Travis would arrive via the studio's private jet midway through the shooting schedule. Private jets and cowboys might seem an odd combination, but Travis figured he could handle the luxury. He'd go through hell to be with Sophia. If he had to adapt to luxury instead, well, there was no law that said life always had to be hard.

He walked up behind Sophia and slipped his arms around her, above her round belly, below her breasts, which had become even more lovely with her pregnancy. "I had a different kind of gift in mind."

"Here in the barn?" she asked, sounding like a sex goddess.

"Like that would be the first time."

Sophia pretended to droop her shoulders in disappointment. "I'm going to have to take a raincheck on that gift. I feel as big as a house this morning."

It was cool in the barn in December, so she wore a fluffy green sweater. Travis noticed that she rubbed her last-trimester belly in a different way today than usual, although the baby wasn't due for three weeks. Maybe the sweater was just extra soft and touchable to her.

Maybe not.

Sophia was adamant that a home birth was the only way to keep her birthing experience private. Her midwife could reach the ranch in a little less than an hour, but Travis didn't find that as comforting as Sophia did. He'd witnessed hundreds of animal births in his life, but Sophia was no animal, and he hoped when the contractions began, she'd change her mind and let him drive her to the hospital. She was no longer placing the baby up for adoption, so secrecy was no longer paramount. Her well-being was.

That was a discussion for next week's appointment with the midwife. Today was Christmas Eve, and he wanted to put a smile on Sophia's beautiful face.

"Close your eyes," he murmured. "Don't move."

He went into Samson's stall and scooped up the black-and-gray puppy he'd hidden there. The pup was four months old and probably fifteen pounds, but it was still a puppy with oversized paws and soft fur.

He placed the soft fur against Sophia's soft sweater. "Happy Christmas Eve."

"Oh! A puppy." Her smile was exactly what he'd hoped for.

For about five seconds.

Then it faded in confusion. "Wait. Is this one of Patch's puppies?"

"Yes. She was returned. I thought you might want to keep her."

"The poor thing. Poor, poor puppy." She buried her face in its fur and burst into tears.

Travis scratched the dog behind the ears. "Baby, the dog is happy. Why aren't you?"

"She was returned because she wasn't good enough, was she?"

"No, Roger just got a job offer in another state, and since he'd only had the pup for a few—"

"You don't have to keep pretending for me." Her tears fell as she kissed the puppy.

Having a fiancée in her final trimester had taught Travis that tears were possible over just about any topic. He wouldn't dismiss every tear as hormones, however, not when he knew the unique challenges Sophia faced.

"Come into the office and sit. You and the puppy." He held the desk chair for Sophia, gave her a tissue from the box he'd learned to keep on his desk now that it wasn't just him in the barn, and then he waited to see if she would tell him what was really bothering her.

She did. "You said that everyone wanted Patch's puppies because she's a great cow dog, but for this litter, the father was a mystery. Now the dogs are being returned. It's the father, isn't it? Even with a great mother like Patch, people assume the puppies just aren't good enough. It's so unfair. The puppies didn't do anything wrong."

He crouched down in front of her. "This is the only puppy that's come back to the ranch, and it's because Roger got a job offer in another state. He'll be in an office building all day. That's it. I wouldn't lie to you, Sophia. That puppy is desirable, I guarantee it, whether we know who the father is or not."

"Maybe I should've stuck with my plan to place the baby up for adoption. No one would have known who the biological parents were. The baby would have started life with a clean slate."

That wasn't coming from as far out of left field as it seemed. "You saw the news today that Deezee was convicted of drug trafficking."

She placed one hand on her belly. "That's this poor baby's father. Everyone knows it. Deezee made sure of that, and now he's a felon. How can I make up for that? I'm not that great when it comes to motherhood material. Here's Patch, this legendary cow dog, and even she can't make up for the father. People think her sweet puppies aren't good enough because the f-father—"

"Sophia, listen to me."

Travis hated the son of a bitch who had just been convicted. He wasn't just a drug dealer who'd come to this ranch waving around a gun that could have injured Sophia, but he was the man who'd messed with Sophia's head, too.

The fact that she'd once considered herself in love with Deezee still undermined her confidence in herself.

"You are going to be a great mother. I know this from the bottom of my soul. The fact that you are worried whether or not you'll be good enough for this baby proves that the baby is getting a mom who cares."

He'd tell her that as many times as it took. Deezee had told her crap for five months. Travis was going to tell her truths for the rest of her life. Travis was going to win.

She let go of the puppy with one hand and placed her palm on her belly in that same low place.

Travis covered her hand with his. "No one is ever going to look at this child and think he or she isn't good enough. Deezee chose to sell drugs for money. That's not DNA. That was a choice. Anyone from any parent could make the same choice, or not. Deezee's not going to be around to teach this baby about bad choices. I'm going to be."

He had to stop and clear his throat. Then he thought better of it. Let Sophia see how much he cared.

He looked up at her, and he knew she saw the unshed tears, because she looked a little bit blurry. "I cannot wait to hold this baby. This is the most exciting thing in my world. I may not have contributed any DNA, but I'm going to be part of this child, too. I'm going to teach 'em when to say 'gid-yap' and 'whoa' and not to let their horse step on their reins and to eat their zucchini and to love their mama. That's you."

Sophia's tears subsided. Her breathing was steady and the puppy in her arm was calm. Travis knew their future was bright. Just when Travis had relaxed, Sophia slayed him. "There are a million reasons I'm going to love this baby, Travis, but here's one of the biggest. If it hadn't been for this baby, I would never have come to your ranch. I would never have met you. For that, I will always owe the baby one."

Travis had to bow his head and clear his throat.

"Me, too, Sophia. Me, too."

Under their hands, he felt her stomach draw tight. She wasn't livestock, not at all, but Travis had felt that same kind of contraction in horses and cows. It could pass and not start again for another three weeks. It could be nothing.

"I don't like the look of the weather out there," he said. "Let's put this puppy back in her hay and head back to the house."

Sophia was suddenly keenly interested in rearranging all the ornaments on the Christmas tree.

Travis ran a ranch. He was a big believer that Mother Nature knew what she was doing, but as far as nesting instincts went, this one wasn't particularly useful.

"I'm gonna call the midwife," he said.

Sophia stopped in the middle of switching the locations of a sequined ball and a glass ball. "Why? I feel fine."

Travis nodded. "That's good, baby. Glad to hear it." He dialed the phone.

Outside, the rain turned to sleet.

The radio announced the highways were closed. Travis imagined that children all around Austin were afraid that Santa wasn't going to be able to get his sled through the bad weather tonight. He was afraid the midwife wouldn't.

He was right, damn it all to hell.

In the end, for all the times he'd insisted to Sophia that she wasn't a beast, he was grateful that there were similarities. It made the whole process a little less bewildering. They'd decided ahead of time which bed to use and had plastic coverings and extra sheets prepared. But as Sophia walked around the house rearranging Christmas decorations, he noticed she kept going into the master bathroom, a room he hadn't seen her use once in the four months since he'd begun living with her. It reminded him of a cow who'd kept returning to stand under a particular tree, or a mother cat who'd decided to leave her nice box for a treacherous rafter at the last minute.

He picked up the supplies the midwife had left last week and carried them into the master bathroom.

"I think I'll take a bath," Sophia said. "Then maybe we can watch a Christmas movie on TV."

She got undressed and sat in the tub, but she never turned the water on. She wasn't having any painful contractions for him to time, and the midwife kept telling him on the phone that a first labor could take twelve hours, easily, if Sophia really was in labor. By then, the roads would surely be open.

So Sophia sat in the dry bathtub and Travis pretended that was normal. Then the first painful contraction hit, and poor Sophia went from nothing to full-out labor in no time.

"I don't think this is right," she said, panting to catch her breath.

"Everything is working just like it should."

The pain was scaring her. "But it doesn't always work out. You lose calves every year. We almost lost that kitten—"

But another contraction hit her before the last one ended, and she started trying to do her *hee hee hee* breaths like the online course had taught them.

Another contraction. God, they were coming hard. Fast. His poor Sophia.

Travis kissed her temple, wet as it was from pain and the effort to handle the pain. He knelt next to the tub and kept his arm around her shoulders. He felt so utterly useless.

The contractions left her limp. He could only support her with his arm.

"That calf," she panted. "Mother Nature would have taken that calf and the mother with it if you hadn't been there to help."

"No, baby. You're remembering that wrong."

"You had those straps."

"I didn't have to use them, remember? I just watched and waited, and that baby was born just fine. Your baby is going to be born just fine. It hurts like hell—" and God, he wished he could do something about that "—but it's going just fine."

The contraction started building again, the pain rolling over her as she gripped his hand and tried to breathe.

"That heifer almost died. She couldn't move. She was so tired." Panic was in her voice. She was losing it, the pain was winning, and Travis thought his own heart was going to break a rib, it was beating so hard. She looked too much like her pioneer movie character, the one that had died onscreen.

Help wasn't coming, not until the sleet stopped. Travis couldn't control the weather. He couldn't control Sophia's labor. This was the most important event of his life, the one thing in his life he absolutely had to get right, and he was powerless.

Sophia lifted her head and started panting. *Hee hee hee.*

God bless her. She was still at it. She didn't have a choice. She couldn't quit.

He couldn't, either.

He shoved the fear and the images from that damned movie out of his head as he shifted his position a bit, leaning over the edge of the tub and adjusting his arm to hold Sophia even closer. Her fingers loosened on his as the wave receded.

She plopped her head back onto his arm. "I can't do it. This can't be Mother Nature."

"Listen to me. You are doing everything right."

But she wasted her precious energy to roll her head on his arm, *no, no, no.* "That calf would have died. You had to drag her over to that heifer."

Travis hadn't realized how heavily that still weighed on Sophia. They'd never talked about it before now. This was a heck of a time to talk about anything, but he didn't want her worrying about what could go wrong.

He kissed her temple again. "Everything is going to be okay. When you saw me drag that newborn calf over to the mama, I was just being helpful. She was tired, so I just brought that baby up close to her so she could take care of it. And you know what? When your little baby is born, if you're too tired to move, that'll be okay, too. I'm gonna scoop up that little baby and hold her right here for you." He brought his other arm across her breasts and completed a circle around her, keeping the woman he loved in his arms. "And it's gonna be you and me and that brand new baby, and the three of us are gonna be just fine."

"I'm sorry. This is…just…" She still looked a little unfocused, but not so panicky.

He could feel her body going under the contraction. "You're doing great."

"…just not how we planned it."

"I wouldn't miss this for the world."

"I love you."

He thought he'd never heard the words uttered in a better way. They pierced his soul. "I love you, too."

She let go of his hand and gripped the edge of the tub. The last of that dazed and confused expression lifted as she frowned fiercely. "I think—I feel like I should push. It hasn't been long enough, has it? What time is it? Ohmigod, I'm not kidding. I need to push. Am I supposed to push?"

Travis nodded. "If you think it's time to push, then you should push. I know you're right."

"Okay. Then I'm going to have a baby now."

He dropped one more kiss on her head. "You do that, Sophia. You do that."

And she did.

In record time, in a bathtub on the River Mack ranch on Christmas Eve, Noelle Jackson Chalmers was born, healthy and loved.

Travis wept. No one had ever been given a better Christmas gift.

* * * * *

And don't miss the next book in
Caro Carson's TEXAS RESCUE *miniseries,*
coming in June 2017 from
Harlequin Special Edition.

#2521 A FORTUNE IN WAITING
The Fortunes of Texas: The Secret Fortunes • by Michelle Major
Everyone in Austin is charmed by architect Keaton Fortune Whitfield, the sexy new British Fortune in town—except Francesca Harriman, waitress at Lola May's and the one woman he wants in his life! Can he win the heart of the beautiful hometown girl?

#2522 TWICE A HERO, ALWAYS HER MAN
Matchmaking Mamas • by Marie Ferrarella
When popular news reporter Elliana King interviews Colin Benteen, a local police detective, she had no idea this was the man who tried to save her late husband's life—nor did she realize that he would capture her heart.

#2523 THE COWBOY'S RUNAWAY BRIDE
Celebration, TX • by Nancy Robards Thompson
Lady Chelsea Ashford Alden was forced to flee London after her fiancé betrayed her, and now seeks refuge with her best friend in Celebration. When Ethan Campbell catches her climbing in through a window, he doesn't realize the only thing Chelsea will be stealing is his heart...

#2524 THE MAKEOVER PRESCRIPTION
Sugar Falls, Idaho • by Christy Jeffries
Baseball legend Kane Chatterson has tried hard to fly under the radar since his epic scandal—until a beautiful society doctor named Julia Fitzgerald comes along and throws him a curveball! She may be a genius, but men were never her strong suit. Who better than the former MVP of the dating scene to help her out?

#2525 WINNING THE NANNY'S HEART
The Barlow Brothers • by Shirley Jump
When desperate widower Sam Millwright hires Katie Williams to be his nanny, he finds a way back to his kids—and a second chance at love.

#2526 HIS BALLERINA BRIDE
Drake Diamonds • by Teri Wilson
Former ballerina and current jewelry designer Ophelia Rose has caught the eye of the new CEO of Drake Diamonds, Artem Drake, but she has more secrets than the average woman. A kitten, the ballet and *lots* of diamonds might just help these two lonely souls come together in glitzy, snowy New York City.

HSECNM1216

*Everyone in Austin is charmed by
Keaton Whitfield Fortune, the sexy new British Fortune
in town—except Francesca Harriman, the one woman
he wants in his life! Can he win the heart of the
beautiful hometown girl?*

*Read on for a sneak preview of
A FORTUNE IN WAITING
by Michelle Major, the first book in the newest
miniseries about the Fortune clan,*
***THE FORTUNES OF TEXAS: THE SECRET
FORTUNES.***

"The dog wasn't the silver lining." He tapped one finger
on the top of the box. "You and pie are the silver lining. I
hope you have time to have a piece with me." He leaned
in. "You know it's bad luck to eat pie alone."

She made a sound that was half laugh and half sigh.
"That might explain some of the luck I've had in life. I
hate to admit the amount of pie I've eaten on my own."

His heart twisted as a pain she couldn't quite hide
flared in those caramel eyes. His well-honed protective
streak kicked in, but it was also more than that. He wanted
to take up the sword and go to battle against whatever
dragons had hurt this lovely, vibrant woman.

It was an idiotic notion, both because Francesca had
never given him any indication that she needed assistance
slaying dragons and because he didn't have the genetic
makeup of a hero. Not with Gerald Robinson as his father.

But he couldn't quite make himself walk away from the chance to give her what he could that might once again put a smile on her beautiful face.

"Then it's time for a dose of good luck." He stepped back and pulled out a chair at the small, scuffed conference table in the center of the office. "I can't think of a better way to begin than with a slice of Pick-Me-Up Pecan Pie. Join me?"

Her gaze darted to the door before settling on him. "Yes, thank you," she murmured and dropped into the seat.

Her scent drifted up to him—vanilla and spice, perfect for the type of woman who would bake a pie from scratch. He'd never considered baking to be a particularly sexy activity, but the thought of Francesca wearing an apron in the kitchen as she mixed ingredients for his pie made sparks dance across his skin.

The mental image changed to Francesca wearing nothing but an apron and—

"I have plates," he shouted and she jerked back in the chair.

"That's helpful," she answered quietly, giving him a curious look. "Do you have forks, too?"

"Yes, forks." He turned toward the small bank of cabinets installed in one corner of the trailer. "And napkins," he called over his shoulder. Damn, he sounded like a complete prat.

Don't miss
A FORTUNE IN WAITING by Michelle Major,
available January 2017 wherever
Harlequin® Special Edition books and ebooks are sold.

www.Harlequin.com

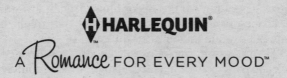

JUST CAN'T GET ENOUGH?

Join our social communities
and talk to us online.

You will have access to the latest
news on upcoming titles and special
promotions, but most importantly,
you can talk to other fans about your
favorite Harlequin reads.

Harlequin.com/Community

Facebook.com/HarlequinBooks

Twitter.com/HarlequinBooks

Pinterest.com/HarlequinBooks

THE WORLD IS BETTER WITH

Romance

Harlequin has everything from contemporary, passionate and heartwarming to suspenseful and inspirational stories.

Whatever your mood, we have romance when you need it, wherever you are!

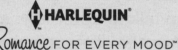

H HARLEQUIN®

A *Romance* FOR EVERY MOOD™

www.Harlequin.com

#RomanceWhenYouNeedIt